ABOUT THE BOOK

Dumped, dejected, and dumbfounded, Nick suddenly found himself without a compass or a clue. Giving Laura up was the last thing Nick wanted, but he had to leave, set himself ablaze, and rise up again. He set off to explore America on the road, keeping journals and writing letters that he thought no one would ever read.

The Road Letters is a personal journey through the abyss of relationship loss, self-discovery, understanding, and rising up from the ashes. An emotional rollercoaster simulated by viewing the world and sharing the pain, sacrifice, and triumphs of Nick Anthony. In an attempt to save himself, Nick battles his instincts, lets go of everything he knows to be true. He strives to make sense out of life and to find a way back to the love of his life.

The story is told through letters and pictures that Nick sends Laura, his lost love, and is supplemented with his transcribed audio and written journal entries. Along the way, he re-establishes old relationships with family and friends, photographs the spectacular countryside, meets interesting people, and faces varied situations—learning about life along the way. He finally returns home after months for one last chance at love.

Cover/interior pictures and design by Philip Ribaudo. Interior layout designed by Philip Ribaudo and Mindy Roberts.

the road
letters

a memoir

by Phil Ribaudo

Copyright ©1999—2006 Philip Ribaudo

Fnx Publications

COPYRIGHT

the road letters by Philip Ribaudo©1999-2006

Copyright ©1999-2007 by Philip Ribaudo
All rights reserved. Printed in the United States of America. No part of this book may be used or reproduced in any manner whatsoever without written permission from the author except in the case of brief quotations embodied in critical articles and reviews.

Information:
fnx@feenx.com
www.theroadletters.com
The feenX store:
www.theroadletters.com/zen

The Library of Congress Control Number:2006934212
The Library of Congress Cataloging-in-Publication Data
Ribaudo, Philip

The Road Letters: 1. **Biography** & **Memoirs**-Memoir. 2. **Travel-United States**-General. 3. **Family** & **Relationships**-Love&Romance-Family-Friendships 4. **Self-help**-Presonal Growth. 5. **Cooking**-General. 6. **Photography**-General. 7. **Music-Criticism**-General. 8. **Philip Ribaudo**

ISBN # 1-59330-429-3

AUTHORS RIGHT

Embellishment

Oxford American Dictionary

embellishment |em_beli sh m_nt|

noun

a decorative detail or feature added to something to make it more attractive : architectural embellishments.

- a detail, esp. one that is not true, added to a statement or story to make it more interesting or entertaining.
- the action of adding such details or features.

TABLE OF CONTENTS

About the Book	i
Suggested Song List	x
Picture and Recipe Index	xi
Acknowledgments	xi
Dedication	xiii
Epigraph	xiv
Preface	xv

Part I: The Reason

Chapter 1 ......Drowning	1
Chapter 2 ......The Meeting	15

Part II: Going Home

Chapter 3 ......Going Back Home	25

Part III: Journals and the Road Letters

Chapter 4 ......First Steps	33
Chapter 5 ......Atlanta Brave	51
Chapter 6 ......Leavin' Leeseana	67
Chapter 7 ......Deep in the Heart of Texas	91
Chapter 8 ......Madman on the Highway	103
Chapter 9 ......Mile High	129
Chapter 10 ......Bakery and Brewery	135
Chapter 11 ......Green Table	141
Chapter 12 ......FeenX	153

TABLE OF CONTENTS

Chapter 13	Tempe Tempe Tempe	163
Chapter 14	The Road	175
Chapter 15	Revelations	193

Part IV: Home

Chapter 16	Home	199
Chapter 17	The Wedding	203
Chapter 18	The Call	207
Chapter 19	My Mother	213
Chapter 20	Game Day	217

Part V: The Date

Chapter 21	The Wait	221
Chapter 22	Love	233

Part VI: Conclusion

Epilogue	241

Author's Note	245
Disclaimer	246
Glossary	247
Character List	249
Index	251
About the Author	254

SONG LIST

The Road Letters Arrangement ©Ribaudo2001
This suggested SongList follows the path of the story and could be enjoyed while reading.

17 Songs from the Road

"Enter Sandman"—Metallica

"About a Girl"—Nirvana

"Nothing"—Edie Brickell

"Déjà Vu"—CSN

"Under the Bridge"—Red Hot Chili Peppers

"Long, Long, Way from Home"—Foreigner

"Alive"—Pearl Jam

"Livin' on the Edge"—Aerosmith

"Wherever I may Roam"—Metallica

"Romeo and Juliet"—Indigo Girls

"Take It Easy"—Eagles

"The Boys Are Back in Town"—Thin Lizzy

"Seven Days"—Sting

"Brown Eyed Girl"—Van Morrison

"Piano Man"—Billy Joel

"Wonderful Tonight"—Eric Clapton

"Sunshine of Your Love"—Cream

PICTURES AND RECIPES INDEX

Pictures

Reflective Tribute	46
Tea for Two	65
The Band	86
The Capitan	100
Carlsbad Caverns	128
Sand and Totem	134
Clap Hands! Clap Hands!	139
Hello, Cacti	151
Cathedral Rock	162
Damsel's Tower	173
The Reason People Climb to the Top	187

Recipes

Chicken Soup	49
Filet Mignon au Poivre	66
Bananas Foster	87
Fettucine Alfredo	101
Lentil Soup	152
Spaghetti and Meatballs with Tomato Sauce	174
Linguini with Broccoli Rabe, Garlic, Sausage, and Cannellini	188

ACKNOWLEDGMENTS

I would like to thank everyone who made writing this story possible, including my family, teachers, friends, critics and skeptics. Thank you all.

To my mother, who taught me to be careful, and my father, who told me I should take some risks. To my grandparents, who gave me the other side of my brain. To Mark, to whom I wanted to prove I could do it. To Matt, who I wanted to inspire and show that anything is possible if you just do it. To Margaret, thanks.

To Jen, the love I lost, because I chose to go forward with this project. To Judy and Holly, Peter and Nancy, Bob and Pam, Beto, and Tom and Amy, thank you for providing hope and a roof. To John, Mike, Ray, and Heff—just because. To Gil, who saved my life.

To Scott Peck, who I've met; he inspired me, he showed me a very different map, and he challenged me to go out and make a difference.

To the writing process and to all my *editors*—everyone who helped with my manuscript: Margaret Ribaudo, Melinda Roberts, Dr. Patti Lorimer Lundberg, Jenn Anderson, Matt Calderisi, and B. M. Ribaudo.

To Mindy, whose faith in me and belief in this story gave me the strength to push this boulder over the top. Thank you Mindy, for your love, technical effort, and emotional support that helped me complete this part of the journey.

To the real heroes! Not the people we put on pedestals for various reasons, but the real people who go out there everyday and cope with real life.—You're the true heroes, the rock stars.

For Lisa

"I shall be telling this with a sigh

Somewhere ages and ages hence:

Two roads diverged in a wood, and I—

I took the one less traveled by,

And that has made all the difference."

—Robert Frost, 1916

"The Road Not Taken"

Preface

✦ ❊ ✢ ■ ✸

    There are always three sides to every story—your side, my side, and somewhere in the middle (where the truth may lie). This memoir is my side…

    This story is told through the eyes of a young man in love. From the beginning naïve Nick truly believed that everything was going to be fine.

Part I

The Reason

Chapter 1

Drowning

I couldn't breathe. I was struggling, trying to wake up from one of those bad dreams—you know, the kind of dream that doesn't let you wake up. I wished it was only a bad dream. But it wasn't a dream at all; there was no waking up; the nightmare was very real.

My father had retired that day, and to celebrate the many years of dedicated service he gave away to corporate America we were going to dinner as a family. Albeit, it didn't have anything to do with my father or his retirement; it just happened on the same day.

Laura called me at work. She wasn't coming to the "celebration." She needed to see me immediately after my father's dinner. She threw down those four dreaded words, "We need to talk," at my feet. You know the sky is falling when you hear that. I went over to her apartment with my Work Smirk in full bloom.

A Work Smirk is the look you get on your face when you're having a great time at a raging party and realize that you have to stop enjoying yourself because you have to leave to go to work; a depressing, sickly, fun-and-games-are-over type of feeling.

From the moment I put my key in the lock and kissed Laura hello, I knew I was in for a rough night. Laura wasted no time at all; wasting time wasn't her style.

She led in with, "There are a lot of things going on in my head right now."

"Oookay," I said, unsure of the direction of the conversation.

"I don't know what I want out of life anymore," she went on. "I still love you, and that's what makes this so hard. I'm not sure whether you're the one I want to spend the rest of my life with." She concluded with, "I don't know whether we should continue to see each other."

BAM!

At the time, I would have never guessed that breaking up was a possibility; it jumped out at me like an unexpected stop sign. Inch by inch, paralysis crept through my entire body.

In the amount of time it takes to flush a toilet, a four-year relationship was over—just like that. Sure we both had our separate apartments, but we spent most of our time together in the same one—hers. I stood there frozen in the moment, unable to think or move.

There was more: "There's no spark in our life right now, I know that I love you and we're best friends, but I'm confused. Maybe we should take a little break from each other."

"How can you think about breaking up right now?"

She said, "That's just it, I feel as though I should be leaning on you right now, but I'm not. I feel as if I need to deal with this by myself, and I feel like there is something wrong with that." Laura looked up at me with teary red eyes and pleaded to be let off the hook of guilt. "Please don't hate me!"

"Hate you? I don't hate you, I love you, I want to be with you and nothing else matters."

Her wilted composure sprang back to life. "Other things do matter, and that's part of the problem."

Without blinking, out of fear of missing some clue, tears streamed down my face. I was so blindsided—I didn't have the strength to fight it or to fight her. I had to leave; I had to get out of there. I thought that if I left, maybe she'd call me back, maybe she'd realize the mistake she was making. After all, she did say she loved me and didn't want to hurt me.

As I had hoped, when I did try to leave, she wouldn't let me. But it was because I was so upset—only because I was so upset.

I didn't know what to say or do. We were both upset. I held on tightly to the fact that she didn't let me leave. Maybe she would rethink the entire situation that night and change her mind in the morning.

We sat on the big couch that crowded her small one-bedroom apartment and watched television—my mouth was dry. Laura held and caressed my hand, the way you do when you're holding something of great value and you know you can't keep it forever. You hope something magical will rub off onto your soul before you have to give it back. We went to bed and cuddled all night long, as we always did, except that night my mind worked overtime trying to solve the puzzle. It was impossible to relax enough to benefit from a full REM cycle. I tried to figure out what was going on.

How this could be happening when we were still so close? We hadn't been fighting or not getting along. We loved and enjoyed the same pleasures—conversation, movies, life, food, and drink. We had been best friends for four years; we lived together half the time, spoke with each other every day—every single day. We had been through a lot—both apart and together.

Laura was a smart, beautiful, and *independent* woman. She was a woman to be reckoned with and revered. An independent woman can be very sexy, seductive, and desirable, yet tantalizing at the same time. When we were together, it was fucking amazing.

We could hang out with each other, our friends and families, or we could each do our own thing with our own friends or families, without the petty jealousies or insecurities that we had both encountered in the past.

We could talk about anything together—no subject was off-limits. We would banter for hours about the silliest things. Laura wasn't even afraid to roll up her sleeves and get down and dirty in debate. She understood that just because we might have a different view on an issue, it wasn't personal. We could believe in different things and still believe in each other.

Laura had a strong, raspy voice. Entrancing. Her laugh was so contagious that mere mortals couldn't help but laugh along with her and feel good when they heard it. Laura had a great sense of humor, and she could even laugh at some of the over-the-edge, dark comedy that I enjoyed at times. Even if the subject wasn't politically correct, she could still find the humor.

Laura could hang with The Boys. The Boys, my very best friends, accepted and loved her—a bit of a rarity. And, in this case, their acceptance wasn't their standard two-faced kind of thing, either. It was routine for The Boys to talk with each other openly about all the girlfriends who didn't measure up to our impossible standards—.

You know, the kind of fun but hurtful things said among buddies.

It was a way of publicly knocking each other down a few feet. Remarks about whose girlfriend wasn't that pretty or who had crooked teeth, or whose girlfriend was a bitch, or whose girlfriend wasn't that smart, or whose girlfriend made their boyfriend feel as though he were in shackles—the proverbial "ball and chain." In some of the cases, the girls actually *did* deserve it, and The Boys deserved abuse for bringing those girls out in the first place. There was unwritten, self-inflicted pressure put on all The Boys to bring someone really special to the table, or you would feel the wrath— "FFFO (Friends Fuck Friends Over.)" The difference between most guys and most girls is that guys will come straight out and make comments to each other, while girls will either think some witchy thing or say it behind their girlfriend's back and then believe they're more proper for taking that approach.

The Boys didn't have any bad things to say about Laura and, as far as I was concerned, that was a home run for me. The fact that they genuinely liked her made me feel as though I had found someone truly special. Laura was clearly the best-looking girlfriend in our little circle, she was cool with my friends and my friends were cool with her. The fact that Laura was also my best friend made me feel like a true winner. What more could a guy want?

My favorite line from The Boys was, "How the hell did a little meatball like you end up with a girl like Laura?"

Did I mention Laura's eyes? People can talk about a girl's legs, breasts, or ass all day, but it all starts with her eyes. Eyes are probably the first things you notice. Maybe you catch her looking at you, or she catches you looking at her, and your eyes meet and lock on. The point comes when you look deeply into a girl's eyes, I mean really deeply, you can touch her soul, feel her spirit—actually meld with her being and become one. Laura's eyes were like tractor beams—drawing me deep into her soul every time. Complete this picture with her dynamite smile, and I was her zombie.

On top of all these qualities, Laura had a really cool attitude and outlook. She gave me the freedom to do my own thing with The Boys without throwing a lot of guilt my way—killing *independent Nick*, as another ex was successful at doing.

Everyone loved Laura. It took some time, but eventually even my parents couldn't resist loving her.

As much as I tried to relax and pretend that this was a dream, I couldn't. It really was happening!

The morning after my heart was choked, I woke up in a dazed funk. Actually, I didn't sleep very much at all. Laura, dressed and ready for work, sat on the bed next to me. She kissed my face and held my hand. The possibility that the night before was only a bad dream popped into my head.

Laura said with a smile, "You are so *cuddable* in the morning."

Testing the waters, I asked, "So why are you doing this?" But the dream quickly melted into a muddy puddle of reality.

Laura's lips quivered, and her eyes welled up with tears, rolling down her well-sculpted cheeks. She started crying because she was saying goodbye. It wasn't the "I'll see you next week" goodbye, it was the "Have a nice life" goodbye. The kind of goodbye that's forever.

"Please don't be mad at me," she said. "The part that hurts me the most is knowing that I'm hurting you."

"So don't," I said. "You don't have to do this."

"I'll always love you." She wiped the tears from her eyes. "I have … to go…. I … can't …. I … have to… go."

She put my hand down and walked out of her apartment and out of my life. I yelled from the bed as I heard her unlock the door, "Laura! I love you, Laura!" The door closed and I heard her, from the other side, lock the locks. My whole world started spinning out of control. That's what happens when you hold on to something too tightly.

I was on the verge of losing my mind. I didn't know up from down; it was like being under water with my eyes clamped shut. I was confused—scattered in my thoughts. I was drowning.

I didn't believe for a minute that Laura's condition had anything to do with the breakup. Laura was strong, stubborn, and determined. She never missed a day of work. She never complained; she never showed any side effects. You would have never known that there was anything wrong with her. I always figured that we would overcome and conquer her illness together, that she would be cured, and that we would go on with the rest of our lives—together.

Everyone tried to convince me that the last thing they would do if they were in the same situation is shut out their best friend the way Laura did. I guess it's possible that in the back of her mind Laura thought I might leave her and figured that it would be better to leave than to be left.

But I wasn't going anywhere.

In the days and weeks that followed, like a mental patient, I tried calling Laura on the phone but she never answered or returned my calls. Half the time I left messages, and the other half I hung up because I didn't want to look like a lunatic even if I had been acting like one. I didn't want to call her at work because I figured she would think that it wasn't fair, but eventually I had no choice.

The first time I got in touch with Laura was at work. I was really nervous, and I wasn't prepared for her to actually come to the phone, so the conversation didn't last very long. The only thing I did manage to get out of her was that she wasn't going to see me. I asked whether it was okay to call her. She said it was okay but that she didn't want me to call everyday.

In preparation for our second conversation, I made a list of some things to talk about so that when I got nervous and my mind went blank, I could still talk even if I couldn't think.

I called Laura again at work, and before I knew it I was taking the conversation to places I probably shouldn't have. Laura tried to dispel my notion that this was about her seeing someone else. I really didn't know for sure. I couldn't imagine what else could have given her such strength. I mean, why else was she able to call it quits, cold turkey, the way she did?

"I wonder if there is something more out there," she said. Which made me wonder what the "something more" was.

I told her I had some clothes at her apartment that I needed. I tried to claw my way back into her life anyway I could.

"I think you should pick up your clothes when I'm at work." She wasn't ready to see me—it hurt too much and brought back too many memories. Laura was trying to forget me.

Then Laura said, as if I were the one devastating her, "This is hard for me as well. I can't say that I don't miss you, but I'm okay with us being apart. I just need time for myself."

I've used that line before, and I knew just where it would lead. Now I was the one being told—I knew the results and I didn't like it at all. Laura had complete control of the situation and I had nothing—my *hand* was gone. That drove me crazy.

"You should use this time to find yourself," she said.

"I miss you and want to be there for you any way I can."

"You can be there for me by taking care of yourself."

Losing the battle, I told her, "I want my friend back, I love you so much." My voice trembled.

Crying, Laura told me that I was just trying to get her upset, and it wasn't fair; she was at work and work was stressful enough.

"I can't take it anymore!" she said and hung up.

I'll admit I was trying to get her to remember how she felt about me, although I wasn't trying to push her to the point of hanging up on me.

I never could handle *the hang up*. I called her right back to say goodbye and to tell her that I loved her. Laura was still crying. She told me that she just couldn't keep going through this, and then she hung me again.

Laura had just taken my *other hand*—I was useless, and I was extremely angry.

My list of topics to discuss did help lengthen the painful conversation, and the bottom line was that Laura decided we wouldn't be seeing that much of each other.

I took some solace in the fact that Laura called back later to say that she was sorry about hanging up on me. But she also demanded that I promise not to make her feel bad the way I did earlier if we were to continue to talk with each other. I told her that I was sorry.

She was in total control.

I was scratching and clawing—the stink of desperation was all over me, and the harder I tried, the worse the smell got. It's funny how you can't smell how bad it is when you're sitting in it, but the stink is so obvious and pathetic to everyone else.

Nothing in this world is worse than uncontrollable, undisciplined, desperate attempts to get back something you can't have—nothing I can think of anyway. My attempts to see her—get to her heart—were pathetic at so many conscious levels that it was frightening.

I waited hopelessly for a call, a message on my machine, a sign that Laura was still out there—something, anything. I couldn't concentrate at work. I couldn't eat. I couldn't think. The one thing that I could do was sleep—and I slept all the time, but never when I wanted to.

First days, then weeks had gone by without any contact from Laura. After all my failed requests, I was compelled to try again.

I had just gotten out of a promising job interview. I was somehow trying to prove to Laura that I could be on a better career path than I had been on. A corporate career that could promise the world, and then she would be so impressed. Maybe that was what she wanted.

The only thing I was completely sure of in terms of the corporate scene was that every corporate job was filled with political bullshit and hypocrisy. As much as I was convinced that the corporate machine would turn me and burn me again, I had to try something. I was a cynic to begin with, and this current situation with Laura only proved my worldview to be accurate.

When I got out of the interview that had gone exactly as I expected, I felt pretty high about my acting skills and performance. I did have a nice suit on, and I told them all the crap that they wanted to hear.

I thought it might be a good time to *go to Vegas* and try talking to Laura again.

It had just started to drizzle as I called Laura from a pay phone outside a gas station. I figured I would avoid small talk. I'd ask Laura to meet me for a drink. What was the harm in one drink?

I'd play it cool, talk fast and it should be no big deal. So, Laura hadn't agreed to see me in over a month. So what? Laura shot me down like ducks in a barrel every time I'd attempted any contact—this time would be different. I felt cool and confident; I would not be defeated.

"Hi Laura, it's Nick, how are you? How about meeting me out for a drink?"

"I can't, I'm busy," she said. "I'm going to visit my sister in Chicago in the morning and I have to pack."

"For Pete's sake, Laura, it doesn't take that long to pack. I don't understand what the harm in seeing me could be."

"I'm not ready to see you, it would be too painful," she said, in the mantra that she forced me to get used to.

"What the hell are you talking about, for Pete's sake, you love me, what's this talk about pain?"

"I have to take care of myself and you need to take care of yourself."

"You can take care of yourself, and we can still be friendly, for Pete's sake. There, now you've gotten me to say 'for Pete's sake' three times, and I never use that expression."

She laughed and said, "I know."

Okay, I got a laugh—good start—that was the break I needed, I thought.

"I don't think we should spend time together right now," she said, "and I thought you were going to pick up your clothes."

So much for my lucky break.

I felt the flat spin of an out-of-control fighter jet coming on. I could see the one-two punch coming my way, and I just stood there, powerless to defend myself or even get out of the way. First, a left jab to set me up and then a right cross to my cheek—knocking my mouthpiece flying.

"I ... I ... I ... picked up most of them," I stammered like a sap. I was so pathetic; I really thought this was a temporary situation. I rapidly started losing my cool.

Laura came across as though she were finally tired of playing this little game, and she just wanted it to be over.

"You should have picked them all up; I would have. You might as well, and you should also pick up any CDs or anything else that belongs to you in my apartment."

Bolo punch to the stomach, taking my breath away.

Having some possessions at her apartment kept my presence in her life alive. Now, she was in a rush to put me out like a dog.

The only thing Laura hadn't asked for was her apartment key. I hoped she wouldn't ask for the key—*please, anything but the key.*

"I think you should see other women."

Well, when I hoped for anything but the key, I meant anything but the key and anything worse than the key. Perfect. That was fucking great. I should be seeing other women! Did this mean that

Laura was seeing other men? I literally scratched the back of my head off trying to figure out what else could give her such strength to be doing this.

I was still standing at the pay phone; it was starting to rain harder. Then it began to pour. These pathetic scenes always take place during a downpour making the mood complete. Then, the operator asked for more money. While I was groveling with Laura at a pay phone in the rain she drops that I should start seeing other women.

Laura didn't ask for the key back, but this was much worse than the key—she didn't need the key back, she could just have the locks changed. Just like the dream about falling off a cliff—I approached the slippery slope and as much as I tried to resist, in slow motion, I kept slipping and falling, nearing the edge. Desperation was getting the best of me—again.

"Does this mean you are done with me?" I asked, trying to get some sympathetic response.

"You don't have to put it like that," she said as though I were offending her.

"How would you put it?" I asked. "I'm not done with you, and I'm not giving up!"

"Well—I am...." Laura said, with fatality and finality.

Ooo–fa!

I was lip-deep in shit trying to prevent myself from being sucked under.

"That's just for now ... not forever," I said.

"All I can see is now," she said. "Now *is* forever."

I was on that amusement park ride that spins in a tight circle so fast that the g-force pins you against the wall and you are paralyzed. I tried to reach for the ejection lever by opting for a misdirection—perhaps a simple topic would change the direction of this conversation.

I tried to get back on track with, "How are you doing?"

"I'm fine and you will be fine, too, without me—I know you will. I can't talk any longer; I have a lot of work to do."

"Laura, meet me for a drink."
"I can't."
"One drink."
"I can't."
"Just one drink, I'm all dressed up and everything," I said pleading.
"No, I just can't; I have to be up early," she said.
I whined on. "Please! I need to see you before you leave, I haven't seen you in a month; I hate this! Please! I miss you!"
"I know."
"I love you."
"I know."
"Don't you miss me?"
"I do, but I'm fine, and you will be, too; I know you will."
I fought back reverting to a child.
"So that's it, just like that, out with the garbage, four years all completed in a five-minute telephone conversation, thank you very much!"
Silence on both ends.
Everything that I didn't want to say or do—complete with shaky voice; everything I'd been holding back—how rancid I was; everything that came out of my mouth pushed her farther away, I knew it and yet I couldn't stop it; I couldn't control myself.
"I have to go," she said. "You promised me that you wouldn't do this to me."
"I'm sorry, I'm sorry, I'm sorry!" On top of everything, I was apologizing. I tried to scratch my way back into her life any way I could.
I was a man—with no pride.
Bloodied and beaten, hoping for a rematch someday, I said, "Have a safe trip, tell your sister I said hello."
"I will—bye," she said.
"Bye," was the only word I had left.
I stood bent over in the downpour, completely twisted in pain, wishing I had never called, my tears blending with the rain.

Nothing would have changed if I didn't call, but as soon as I stuck my head out—Wham! Every time!

Thank God for Gabrielle. Gabby is my brother's wife and chief headshrinker, she was the one who talked me down off the ledge that day. If I couldn't tell whether I was being irrational or was rationalizing everything, I could lie down on Gabby's couch and have my head shrunk. Gabby talked me off many ledges. There weren't many people that I could talk to about this particular disaster in my life. Friends and family were sympathetic to my pain, but they wanted a swift, simple resolution to return my happiness. Everyone's speedy simplistic solution and all I ever heard—"Move on!" "It's time!" "Give up!" "Quit!" Quitting and giving up wasn't part of my plan. The hardest part for me was that I just couldn't give up. In my mind, giving up would have been more painful than continuing to try.

Could I continue to live like this? I had to do something, because life like this wasn't working. Something had to change. I needed to break away from this rut, this curse that I believed in—but how? What was life all about? Did I need to leave her, in an attempt to get her back?

Regardless, I needed to get some distance. I needed to show Laura that I could move on and that I wasn't a pathetic sap. I needed to find a way to give her the space she needed and a way for me to persevere. I needed to get my identity back. I needed to take risks again.

I had no choice—I had nothing more to lose, the abyss was staring me in the face. I had to find out what I was made of and what life was all about. It was a risky scheme and a backward approach, but it seemed to satisfy all the requirements.

I had to leave.

My plan was simple, yet frayed around the edges, in its early stage. Eventually, I ironed out the wrinkles so that I appeared to be somewhat sane. I knew it took all of my parents' strength to be supportive and understanding, because it went against everything my mother drilled into my head for the last twenty-eight years of my life. "Have a good job, have security, make money, don't take risks, be safe," was my mother's mantra.

My estimated departure date was supposed to be the first of the year. Fresh starts, new beginnings—that sort of idea.

There are many details to consider when you leave on an open-ended ticket. I needed to plan out my stops, get financially organized, and quit my job—put the phone on the hook.

As it turns out, the planning phase was just the therapy that I needed to get through the early stages of delirium.

Chapter 2

The Meeting

From time to time, I would break down and try to get in touch with Laura.

Unexpectedly, in late October a couple of months before my trip was to begin, for some unknown reason and after countless futile attempts, Laura finally agreed to see me. I was glad to have an opportunity to tell her about my planned journey in person. I wanted her to know; I needed her to know.

I wasn't sure exactly why Laura had agreed to see me after eight weeks of shutting me down, but she did. Imagine, after four years of being together, she kept me in complete darkness for eight straight weeks. My neurosis was very active and I kept asking myself: Why was she willing to see me now? How was she going to chop my legs out from under me this time?

Of course, I expected and planned for the worst, but somewhere, in a small corner of my mind, I hoped and prayed for a little crack in her armor. From the beginning, I thought Laura refused to see me because she was afraid that if she saw me, she would realize that we should be together and that wasn't part of her plan. None of this made any sense.

Maybe Laura would finally have the guts to tell me about her new boyfriend. To make a point, I even thought she would bring him to meet me, so that I would finally leave her alone and stop calling.

Nothing was beyond my imagination. My dreams were all recurring nightmares. I dreamed that Laura would introduce me to the new boyfriend I had rationalized into existence—the person who took my place because he was a better man than I was. To end that nightmare, she asked me to be happy for them.

Dream two, a personal favorite, starred the Sheer Attitude Laura saying, "Get over it already, it's been seven months and I'm over you!"

Lastly, there was dream three. In that one, we both sit down at a table, look at each other for some familiar wrinkle, realize we mistook each other for someone we once knew and get up and walk away in opposite directions. So much time has passed that we had nothing to say to each other, everything we shared together had been forgotten, and we were strangers.

I did have a habit of putting myself in places that had pain potential—maybe I was a masochist. I hoped this meeting would be different.

The days before I saw Laura, I came to the realization that I was in a different place mentally than I had been at in the beginning of this mess. And, this time, I had a plan and maps. This time it was about me.

At that point, I had almost everything I needed for my journey—my plans were nearly complete. Despite whatever happened when I saw Laura, I was determined. I was going on this trip.

I reassured Gabby in our pregame pep talk, "Nothing is going to stop me! I am going on this trip despite whatever happens when I see Laura!"

On the outside, I was the Mr. Big Shot, with all the confidence I talked about. I tried to imagine what would happen next, but I didn't have a Magic 8-Ball. And, unfortunately, my imagination had an imagination of its own that never disappointed and loved to play games with me. I tried to imagine every possible scenario with a course of action for each situation. Was my imagination my ally?

Laura and I decided to meet at a place called Company B's, an old haunt where we used to go for beer tastings, with a great

The Meeting

selection of microbrews. They didn't serve Budweiser, or anything mainstream like Bud, and they gave you the stink eye if you even thought about asking for it.

I arrived a *scooch* early. At first, I waited at the bar for Laura; my hands were cold and sweaty. I had forgotten my plans and maps in the car. I had no idea what to expect. I tried to calm myself down. I needed to look good, confident, and to be sure of myself. I needed to be a man, the person she fell in love with. That's the man she needed to see. Although I couldn't show it, I was a train wreck on the inside.

Whatever happened, I had to make sure of one thing: Do not lose my cool!

"Life comes down to a few moments, and this is certainly one of them." That was a speech I gave myself before I entered the arena at any big event in my life.

Laura was late, as usual, so I went to wait by the fireplace near the front lobby. When she did show up, our eyes met and we were both reduced to a puddle of JELL-O. We couldn't help it, and I don't think either of us tried.

Throughout the night we laughed, we cried, we reminisced—it didn't matter who watched us, we were by ourselves in our own little world. I listened to every word she said, searching for clues. I looked for ways to make it all better.

Laura gave me the update on herself, her work, and her family, and I did the same. The biggest change aside from us being apart was that I was leaving in less than two months. Leaving on a journey was something that I knew Laura would be envious of and would love to do herself.

It took all my strength not to go near anything I didn't want to hear or find out about. Albeit, I wanted to know everything, I needed to know everything; I deserved to know—why.

I didn't want the night to be over. We talked as if no time at all had gone by, yet eight weeks had. The night flew by. I ended up more confused about the two of us, but it looked like I was doing the right thing by going on my own journey. Leaving gave Laura the space she needed, and she showed me the excitement and enthusiasm that I loved about her. I was wearing my rose-coloreds, and everything looked wonderful.

It seemed that all the time spent speculating and analyzing was for something.

Laura didn't bring her new boyfriend, and at that moment, I could be pretty confident that this was not about that. She said she needed time to take care of herself, time to figure things out. She couldn't let me be a part of her process and, for me, that was the most frustrating part. I wanted to be there, and she wouldn't let me. I was completely in the dark. I was the typical fool in love—blind.

I had hoped the past eight weeks were just a nightmare, and I would wake up and we could go back to our life, together. I was ready.

Unfortunately, up to that point that night was only a dream, because she woke me up by asking me for the one thing that I held in my possession, the only thing I had left, besides, my spirit—the key.

Laura broke my heart when she asked for the key. She used some lame excuse about her brother needing it so he could get in to paint her apartment. However lame, there was no point in questioning her reason. I just slid the key across the table along with my rose-colored glasses and my heart.

That was the smack back into reality that I needed. After all, I had a journey to go on. It was my destiny, just as I felt she was; only she was unreachable. When we left the bar, I walked Laura to her car in the parking lot. It was a cold night—you could see your breath in the crisp night air. Laura asked me to sit with her while her car warmed up. I brought over my plans and maps from my car to show her while we waited.

I rolled out my huge map and showed her my route with stickers marking all the places I intended to go. I was totally

The Meeting

engrossed in it. When I was finally finished yapping, I looked up to see her reaction—I hadn't noticed it before, but she had been crying the whole time I was talking. The fact that Laura was upset caught me off guard. I didn't understand why she was crying.

Laura had this red line around her lips that she would get when she was sad and teary-eyed.

"Why are you crying?" I asked, hoping I knew the answer.

"Because you're leaving," she said.

In my mind, I just shook my head in disbelief. I didn't get it. I was there the whole time, and Laura hadn't let me near her, and there she sat right next to me, upset that I was leaving.

"I'll be back," I said with a revived confidence. You're going through your shit and I'm going through mine. I'll be back, I'm just going to take a look around, see life, see this country, take pictures of the people, places, and things I can't even imagine—giving you the space you need."

"You're leaving, and I'm going to miss you," she said, which gave me even more hope.

I had more confidence than ever that I was doing the right thing. I wanted to say, "I won't leave, I'll stay here with you," but I knew that wasn't what she wanted. It wasn't what I wanted. It wasn't what we needed.

We hugged, and we cried, and we each said, "I love you."

Even with the new positive energy injected into me, one event broke the moment in our last five minutes together. I massaged her shoulder and touched the nape of her neck and, although she seemed to enjoy it at first, she quickly and adamantly asked me to stop. Nothing was completely smooth. I stopped immediately. At least I had managed to break through, if for only a minute.

We hugged one last time while standing between our cars. As I walked away with my plans and maps, I said, "I'll be back—you have my soul and the key to my heart and I will come home to claim them." Then I said, "Remember, some men dare take—what they want," which was a line used by Ricardo Montalbán in a Star Trek episode, and I used to say it to Laura when we first met.

Laura smiled and said, "I know you will, I'm going to miss you! Be careful! Keep in touch!"

It was cold outside, and a frigid breeze blew right through me. I'm still not sure whether our date had been a dream or reality.

I convinced myself that she still loved me. I thought it was quite obvious, I told myself that, anyway. When we looked into each other's eyes, we touched each other's souls; it was beautiful. I would have never guessed that we would have such a positive evening together. It was close to a perfect night, but I had to keep things in perspective. Laura did ask me to stop rubbing her neck. She did ask for my key. But Laura's guard seemed to be down, she had given me something to sink my hopes into. Was it the gift of the Magi?

I waited a couple of days after our date before I called Laura again. The euphoria from our evening together didn't carry far at all—one phone call took care of that. Laura wouldn't take my calls or see me. Our relationship quickly returned to the way it was before our date, and I quickly, but briefly, returned to a blivet emotionally.

I had been brought right back to the place I had been; it was a familiar place, a place where I didn't want to return. But thank God, it was a place that I'd been before, which somehow made it easier. After all, I was still going on this trip despite whatever happened that night—wasn't I? I was still going to be an explorer in search of the meaning of life, people, and America, right?

Damn straight I was.

Besides, Chico, she gave me her eyes, and the eyes don't lie.

On a snowy January night, before my trip was to begin, and days after my planned departure date, I went out with The Boys to have a farewell cocktail. Jack, Paul, and Richard were all present and accounted for. After a couple of beers and a few dozen laughs we said our goodbyes, and they dropped me off at home. It was a good night.

I walked into my bedroom to do a final check on my packing and noticed that the light on my answering machine was blinking.

The Meeting

I wondered who it could be since I was out with everyone who might call. I was shocked to find her voice on the machine.

My answering machine dominated my life for months as I waited, and prayed, and lived for any message from Laura. Each time there wasn't a message from her on that damned machine, a small piece of us drifted away.

I went through the gamut of emotions over and over again—anger, denial, hopelessness, understanding, and finally giving up. And, not once in this entire mess, did she ever call on her own—not once. But this time, it was Laura's voice on the damn machine and my heart pounded wondering where she would go in the message. Laura's message lasted only about 30 seconds, if it lasted that long, but she did say goodbye and to be careful and to stay in touch. Without warning during her unexpected farewell message, Laura's strong raspy voice cracked briefly. After all my planning, leaving was finally upon me—it was time to go.

Part II

Going Home

Chapter 3

Going Back Home

I had been on the road away from home and the Laura situation for over four months—although it felt as if I had just left. I couldn't believe that it was April and that I was on a plane going back home for a visit.

I was returning to the scene of the crime more than seven months since the mess with Laura began. It probably sounds trite, but in my mind, it *was* a crime that we weren't together. At that point; I was just disenchanted, not bitter.

The reason for my return home was to attend Richard's wedding and I was only staying for the weekend. I knew I would make an attempt to see Laura at some point during the long weekend. Thankfully, I was in a different place than I was when I pulled out of the driveway some four months before.

I had so many positive growth experiences since I left, but there were times that it didn't matter where I'd been, what I'd done, or the fears I had faced. There were times when rejection could slam into me like a freight train, knocking every bit of confidence I had into the next week. From time to time, my insanity would take control. A dull ache would take my hunger away.

I was lucky though, because the insane times didn't happen very often anymore or have the same effect that they once had. When my insanity did return, the pain didn't run nearly as deep. The visits came less frequently and lasted for shorter periods each time—thank God. Nonetheless, it was a familiar feeling that could creep up on me in a second, even when I was careful.

From my roomy bulkhead seat, I looked down at my sandals. I would never wear sandals in my previous life. At that point, I figured *to hell with anyone and everyone who had a problem with my sandals*. Merely traveling on the road gave me the right to wear sandals. I noticed the sandals still had some red sand from Monument Valley falling off them. I smiled—and anyone who has taken a journey would know why.

A new spirit drove me. I hadn't been summoned. I had risen through the ashes; I was a survivor—a true FeenX! I left, and then I returned on my own terms.

The plane was about to take off, I made the sign of the cross as I always do, and I got ready for my favorite part of a flight. The power of a takeoff has always given me a rush.

I looked through the plane's window and, only at that moment, did I fully realize what returning *home* meant.

Home.

I continued to stare through the window mindlessly; everything was out of focus. I tried shaking it off to enjoy the power of the takeoff, but my mind wouldn't let that happen.

I was returning home. Not because I failed, not because I couldn't make it in the world on my own, but for a visit.

I was going to *visit home*—an interesting concept.

I knew that when I arrived home I'd be in the safety of my parents' house, surrounded by the people who meant so very much to me—my family and friends. I knew that they would be so happy to see me and excited to hear about my tales from the road. Soon, I would be sitting around the dinner table with my parents and brothers. My mother would smooth out the tablecloth, making sure that it didn't have a wrinkle in it. After dinner, she would ask, as she always did, "Does anyone want some espresso?" To this day, I still don't understand why my mother asked that question every time; no one ever said "no." We would stay seated, have some espresso, maybe a little Sambuca, some of my grandmother's teacakes, and everything would be fine. That was the home that I missed.

Although I missed home, I didn't miss it enough to call this trip back anything more than it was—just a visit. I started thinking about of all the places I had been and all of the unbelievable things I had seen. If I had never left, I wouldn't have experienced any of those things. I probably would have made excuses the same way that everyone else does: "Someday when I get the time" or "someday when the time is right." The thing about time is that there is never enough of it and it never seems to be right. Our whole life can go by thinking in terms of "someday" or "coulda, shoulda, and woulda." "Coulda, shoulda, woulda," makes for a life of regret and disappointment. You wake up one day asking yourself where the time went, and then you die. Coulda, shoulda, woulda—don't mean shit!

Life isn't a spectator sport; we need to make life happen.

I thought about my friends and how they would pick me up at the airport. My friends would always be the ones who picked me up from somewhere—always with a cooler of beer, rubbing their hands together, and smiling with some scheme that would land us in trouble. That was the home I missed.

These were the same friends that I had in high school, some ten years before, and they were still my very best friends. Many people found our friendship a bit odd or queer because they just didn't understand how it was possible. Our friendships had outlasted all of our marriages and some of our families, for that matter. Most people leave their high school friends behind for the new friends they meet in college or at work.

Somehow, time loses your friends from high school; they get lost in the day-to-day, year-after-year grind that *is* life. Except for an occasional class reunion, at which there never seemed to be enough time to catch up at, most people never see their high school friends. Well, not in my world.

I remembered months before when I first told The Boys that I was leaving to find the meaning of life. I knew what my buddy Jack was thinking: "Don't run away from your problems, your friends are here for you. Running away is for wimps." In some ways, I couldn't blame him for thinking it; I knew it was because he cared. Jack, however, was the Marlboro Man—a water walker, he believed he was a tough guy. And I believed that Jack would wear a cowboy hat and chaps if he thought he could get away with it.

I don't think Jack really understood what I was going through, but at least he was supportive enough not to say what he was thinking, at least not to me. At some level, Jack knew that I had to leave and he thought I would be back in a couple of weeks anyway.

Paul, on the other hand, was more understanding and supportive. He got me a beeper so that The Boys could always get in touch with me while I was on the road. He knew I needed to get some distance.

Paul would say, "You can't see everything life has to offer from behind the wheel of a car in Westchester." Of course, Paul saying this was actually quite ironic, because he would say this from behind his desk, in the same room he grew up in, which just happened to be in his parents' house—in Westchester.

Paul was easier to talk to than Jack, more understanding. Jack was a black-and-white kind of a guy. Jack had no room for any shades of gray in his life or in anybody's life who he cared about. Jack didn't like problems; he needed to fix them as fast as they surfaced. That didn't mean there wouldn't be a lot of spare parts lying around when the job was finished—which was usually the case. But that's a whole other story.

Then there was Richard, who recently was so wrapped up in work and in getting married that he had little time for anyone but Silvia, his lovely wife to be. His wedding was the excuse I needed to return home. If Jack was the Marlboro Man, Richard was the Stoneman. Richard never let anyone know what was going on in his head. When you saw Richard in a bar, it was always the same— he had his arms folded with a beer in his hand and a mischievous smile that looked as though he were up to something suspect. Richard and Paul were stuck in a car somewhere for twelve hours with nothing to do but talk, and Richard didn't even mention the fact that he had asked Silvia to marry him the day before. And, two weeks later, Richard asked Paul to be his best man. What was Richard thinking about for twelve hours? Nobody knows, for sure, except the Stoneman.

Paul's bloviating about life outside our little bubble gave me the confidence I needed to be an explorer. I liked the whole romance of being the explorer—searching and finding new things, seeing and experiencing a world that few people had ventured out to see and meeting the people you would only meet in books and movies. Maybe that sounds a little romantic, but it seems to me that most people live their entire lives in the same towns they grew up in, never going out too far, never experiencing more of what life has to offer. It's easier. It's safer. And it's a shame.

The only reason I had the guts to leave the comforts of home was that my back was against the wall—*again*. Sometimes in life you need your back to be against the wall to force you forward.

I still had five hours of flying time staring me in the face. The flight attendant told me that the in-flight movie was about a pathetic guy struggling to get over his ex-girlfriend and his buddies who try to help him move on, but he just can't get out of his own way when it comes to women. I got the impression that it was some sort of chick flick for guys—he sounded pathetic to me, too. Instead of watching a movie that sounded like I could be the star of, I caught up with my travel journals and relaxed with a glass of wine. I decided early on in my trip to keep journals so that someday I could look back to see where I had been. My journals consisted of composition type notebooks that I could write in when I was in a bed, sleeping bag, or lean-to; letters I wrote to Laura, and an audio journal that I kept on a handheld tape recorder while I drove the lonely roads.

It was an adventure going back to my journals—my ticket to the past. My journals brought me back to where I had been, mentally and physically. It was always funny to see my handwriting in my journals or to listen to my mood on the audiotapes after I had been drinking. My handwriting was always atrocious, and the subject matter was usually pretty funny and outrageous. Plus, in my audiotapes I could relive my buzz through my slurred speech.

Of course, as I pulled the journals from my carry-on bag, the copies of the letters that I wrote to Laura were the first things to fall out.

Yes, I made copies.

I relished my mind as an amazing time machine that could bring me lots of pleasure and just as much pain. My mind could bring me to places I had never been and to places where I never wanted to go to again. I was about to go on one of those journeys of the mind that would bring me consciously to both places. Drinking wine may very well have not been the best thing to do while riding the emotional roller coaster of rereading my letters to Laura, but I had a glass of wine in my hand at the time, so I went with it.

I remember resorting to writing Laura letters, after a phone call that I made to her went horribly awry soon after I shoved off on that stormy day in January. It was back when I was still in Myrtle Beach. I was staying at my parents' condo; I was lucky to have the opportunity because they usually rent it out for the winter. I had only been on my journey for maybe two weeks, and the conversation went something like this:

"Hi Laura," I said, optimistically.

"Oh, hi, I can't talk right now, the president is about to give his State of the Union address and I want to listen to him." She seemed to put a lot of importance into what the president had to say that night.

"Uh, uh, how are you?" I asked

"Good. I can't talk, I have to go—bye," were the nine words she could barely bother to scrape together.

"Bye?" I was so angry. I couldn't handle the rejection and anxiety of actual phone calls after that. So letters were my solution, salvation, and the only sane way to keep Laura with me—and, in some way, me with Laura.

Part III

Journals and the Road Letters

"There are roads we travel and for each of us a journey.
No two paths are exactly the same."

—Annonymous, 1994

Chapter 4

First Steps

Audio Journal from the Car

January 22, 1994
Mood: Hopeful

10:30 a.m.

Testing, testing… Traveling on Kings Highway in Myrtle Beach… Weather is cold, and sunny with cloudy blue skies…

Grand Funk Railroad, "I'm Your Captain" is on the radio.

"I'm getting closer to my home…"

I have to go down to DMV about exchanging my driver's license, car insurance, and license plates; Barefoot Landing for wildlife photos, and the fountain to play around with slow speed photography.

10:42 a.m.

Seems like it would be great to travel on a motorcycle. I don't know why, it just does.

10:57 a.m.

Continuing down the strip in Myrtle Beach passing numerous billboards and businesses. What should I do tonight? Maybe, I should go to Bogart's. Seems like a nice place to eat. Hmm, there's a U-Brew, a homebrew supply place—I should check it out.

11:25 a.m.
Tuesday night is bowling 99 cents a game; maybe I'll do that. Or, Players club has 70-cent beers and $1.25 vodka drinks. So much to do, so much to do…I just don't know.

Creedence Clearwater Revival, "Up around the bend" is on the radio.

"Come on the risin' wind, we're goin' up around the bend."

12:15 p.m.
List of things I need to do:
Check the car to make sure it's fit and ready for the next leg of the trip.
Practice setting up the tent—a dry run.
Take some pictures on the strip tonight—the neon is amazing at night!
Important, important, important—pick up a dictionary!

4:10p.m.
Went to my first pawnshop today—very exciting! I've heard about pawnshops, seen them in movies, but have never actually gone into one. Looks like some deals in there.

Tip: Regarding other people's misfortune: you definitely need to capitalize on misfortune because there's a ton of it everywhere and all for the taking. Right… I'm the bad guy. Isn't that what the insurance business is all about?

First Steps

Written Journal Entry
January 25, 1994

Ugggh! The big let down of the evening.... I just got off the phone with Laura. Fuck her! I've been stressing for days over this phone call. She told me that she had to listen to the president; he was on TV. Who the fuck cares? Since when does Laura care about what the president has to say? Doesn't she care about me, how I'm suffering, how I'm in pain—at all? I've been on the road for weeks now and she doesn't even ask how I'm getting along. She graces me with a couple of words then "good-bye." Do you think she called me after his little speech was over—No! Fuck, no!

Fuck you, Laura! Fuck you! I'm tired of sour emotional letdowns. I feel like the happy puppy dog, wagging my tail, jumping up and down, excited for my master to pat me on the head and love me. Meanwhile, I get kicked across the room when I try to get some affection.

I try to resist feeling this kind of anger toward Laura, but it builds to the point of me bursting. I'm a nervous wreck for weeks at a time, not to mention how I feel just before making a hopeful phone call and then she treats me like an insignificant slug and kicks me across the room. To tell you the truth, I really don't have a choice but to be angry.

I do try to keep in mind how difficult it must be for her, which probably brings me back to reality—but I am only human, and I do take it personally.

I turned the picture of Laura I brought with me upside down so I don't have to see her smiling at me. Sometimes I need to be angry over this whole mess. I think it's only healthy. I don't need to have her picture laughing at me when I need to maintain my anger.

Why?
Why does life end before it begins?
Why do I lose, why can't I win?

> Help end my problems—stop them please!
> Why don't they stop? Why don't they cease?
> Why? Why? Why...
> Why, always me?
> What have I done?
> Why have I done it to me?

Wow, I just recalled that poem from high school. I wrote it back when I was struggling with the daily pressures of *that* part of my life. I think I even entered it into a poetry contest at school. Some of the girls judging the contest were all kinds of concerned that I was going to *hurt* myself. Nothing could be further from the truth.

I need this though ... to help push me forward.

While the president was on TV, I practiced setting up my little blue dome tent right in the middle of the living room of my parents' condo. This guy is amazing—shit just keeps coming out of his mouth and everybody, including me, is enthralled. The charisma he exudes is like a tractor beam—it pulls you in! You know he's playing politics, you know he's taking credit for the invention of oxygen, and you know he's lying to your face, and yet you can't help wanting to believe his every word.

The tent fit nicely as though it were a piece of furniture meant to be in the middle of the living room in the condo. A little bit of sand fell out from under one of the flaps. The sand must have been there from the last time I used it, years ago, when I was still married. The tent was one of the few possessions I was *allowed* to keep. I got the tent. I got the scratches from the bottom of my ex's gravel ridden shoe, which she scraped into the hood of what was then my shiny new car. She preformed that act at my brothers' joint college graduation party, which doubled as the first play date my parents had with Gabby's—it was quite a production! The whole party stopped to watch our confrontation on the front lawn. Funny to think about it now: Angelina, my ex, was cursing up a storm while my parents tried to break it up and my father said, "Come on, Angelina, don't use that kind of language, there are children around." And like the drunk child she was she said, "Fuck you, fuck your whole family, fuck, fuck, fuck!" Another funny part to the story was why she was there in the first place. We were only weeks away from signing the divorce papers. My mother, in her infinite wisdom, still wanting Angelina to be a part of the family and probably hoping that we would get back together, invited her. Besides the scratches on my car, I was also rewarded with the extra big California king-size waterbed. Angelina took the impossible-to-find sheets, of course. To spite her, I slept on the bed without sheets for over a year. I showed her didn't I? Angelina took everything else: TV, couch, wedding presents from both sides, as much of my pride as she could stuff in a truck, my ultimate set of tools, which was in the back of my prized fully restored '69 Buick Electra Deuce-and-a-quarter convertible!—which she also took. She told me on the day we signed the final divorce papers that she sold the car for $1 just to piss me off. Fuck her, too! Fuck'em all! Fuck!

How do two people go from loving, caring, and willing to die for each other to just hoping that each other would die? We share in each other's joys and pains and end up referring to each other by nasty names and taking the hard-to-find fucking sheets for the bed! How do we end up there? How do we let it happen? On top of it, *we* involve all these innocent people in the relationship. The now-involved family and friends have unsolicited time and feelings invested in the people, in the relationship, and then everything is lost in the breakup. It makes it almost not worth it—there is so much to lose for everyone, I don't know why anyone makes the gamble.

It took my parents such a long time to accept my divorce and get over my ex-wife. We were separated for almost a year, and when I told them I was getting divorced they were disjointed with shock. I don't know what they thought the separation was about. And then it took them forever to warm up to Laura. They wanted to believe what they wanted to believe about her, they didn't want me to find anyone else, they didn't want to go through another loss—who knows and who could blame them anyway? Just before the non-acceptance of Laura became a huge issue, my parents came around to love her. Time goes by and washes away the pain to new shores of hope that the next time it will all work out.

I miss the warmth and feel of Laura's skin next to mine. She was so soft and smooth; I could rub my cheek over her cheek for hours. With my lips I would caress her luscious lips and nose and cheek and eyes and back to her lips again. We kissed softly and sweetly. We kissed passionately, we kissed deeply. Sometimes, right in the middle of a soft and sweet kiss, she would request sloppy kisses, and we kissed like animals. It would lead to passionate lovemaking that lasted for hours—it was very hot.

As much as I want to bathe in my anger, I just can't stay mad at Laura for too long. God, I miss what we had together.

I can't sleep. I'm staring at the glowing red numbers of the digital clock getting blurry until each minute changes. I want to call someone, anyone, but it's 1:30 a.m. and even though everyone tells me I can call anytime, I know I can't call them this late.

"When I lay down to go to sleep, I sleep in peace. The Lord alone keeps me perfectly safe." This prayer hasn't let me down before and I'm confident it will help me go to sleep now.

Goodnight...

First Steps—Letter 1
January 26, 1994

Dear, Laura,
I hope this letter finds you well. I figured I would resort to writing you letters to keep you updated about my trip. This way, you can read them whenever you're in the mood, and to tell you the truth, it will be easier on me, as well.

My trip started almost a week behind schedule. I lost some time due to the horrible cold, my back was killing me, and my grandfather had a mild stroke a week earlier. I lost a couple of more days due to the constant snowfall.

When I left, it was snowing and sleeting, but I couldn't wait for the weather any longer. My younger brother, Joe, helped me shove off, and he gave me the teary farewell hug in the driveway. I can still picture him in the slick icy snow, with one hand in his pocket to keep warm and the other waving goodbye.

My car was jammed with everything I could possibly need for my trip; there wasn't room for one more thing. As I drove down Bass Road, the road I lived on for all but five years of my life, that Foreigner song "Long, Long, Way from Home" was on the radio. They sang, "It was a day like any other day..." I thought the words were quite apropos.

Good-bye: home, family, friends, safety, and in my case New York. Ironically, I was leaving my home in New York but in the song the character left his home for New York.

My first quick stop was Delaware, where I met my other brother John, who happened to be there on business. I spent the night at his hotel because his company was paying for it, and why not take advantage of a free night when I didn't know where my next meal was coming from or who would be paying for it? John and I had dinner, played pool, drank beer, got drunk, called his wife, Gabby, shared a room and some good times together. John and I should have spent more time together growing up.

When I left the next day, John told me not to trust anyone along the way and to be careful—a common thread that I've heard repeatedly. As we walked over to my car, John asked, "So where are you going now?"

I said, "I don't know," and we both laughed.

And then I said more seriously, "My first stop is Washington, D.C."

We both stood there not knowing what to say as snow started to fall. He broke the moment and said, "Well, don't expect me to start blubbering or anything like that." That was par for the course for my brother, Mr. Sensitivity.

Amazing, two brothers, the same family and a completely opposite style of saying the same thing—good-bye, be safe, we love you.

I tried to outrun the arctic blast that all the weather people on the news reports kept talking about. Well, in Washington, D.C., it caught up to me. Laura, do you remember all the great times we had there? D.C. is such a great city! I went to all the monuments and museums that we've been to together. As cold as it was when we visited, it was much colder this time.

I love the National Air and Space Museum! I have been going to the NASM since I was in the eighth grade—you can't see everything, and you always see something new and different.

There was a big sign that said, "WHY EXPLORE?" It was over Charles Lindbergh's display. His uniform, the supplies, maps, and basically everything he brought with him on his trip was right there on display, including the Spirit of St. Louis!

"WHY EXPLORE?" Exactly! I went to the Lincoln and Jefferson Memorials, the Washington Monument, and across the blustery cold Mall to the Museum of Natural Art, the U.S. Capitol, U.S. Archives, Supreme Court, and the house that your lying buddy lives in.

I'm telling you, this president is self-serving and can't be trusted, and someday he will get caught. Time tells all, eventually.

It was so cold at one point near the Vietnam Memorial that I got one of those headaches—you know, the kind you get by eating ice cream too fast—imagine, just by standing in the blowing wind. It was so cold I couldn't even feel my fingers, but I still felt great!

I went to this brewpub called Capital City, which made some pretty good beer. I tried winter amber ale—very tasty, with a Vienna sausage and roasted pepper sandwich. Then I had a homemade pretzel with Eleanor's Amber Ale—the better of the two.

While I was there minding my own business, enjoying the beer and people-watching, this guy sat next to me at the bar and said that he just got out of jail for beating up his wife. He told me that he was in the military and always got in fights with the police and people around him. He told me he was in the riots down in Los Angeles. I thought, "What the hell, I'm only five hours away from home and my mother is going to be right already." He could have sat anywhere in this huge restaurant, but he sits down next to me. Is there a sign over my head that says, "Trouble, please sit down, make yourself at home and bother Nick?" I sat there, nodded my head like I was listening a couple of times while trying to look like a tough New Yorker—well, he left me alone anyway.

I'm trying to go to as many brewpubs and taste as many beers across the country as I can.

In D.C., I took many pictures, stayed in my first youth hostel, Washington International, which was unexpectedly clean, warm, friendly, filled with lots of people speaking foreign languages from different countries, backpacking across the U.S.A. I thought it was very interesting that people from other countries were taking advantage of the resources that most people in this country don't even know about.

I was feeling a little overwhelmed and decided not to go out my first night alone. Instead, I started writing a journal of my travels from my top bunk assignment at the hostel.

As it turns out, I stayed in D.C. for only one night, but would have stayed longer if it weren't so cold. The cold made it almost impossible to do anything. Before I left for Myrtle Beach in South Carolina, which was only eight hours away, I braved the cold and took a few more pictures.

I thought by traveling down South the temperature would warm up a little bit, but it seems that this arctic blast froze everything in its path including me. Pearl Jam's "Alive" was playing on the radio when I left D.C.

It was 16 below zero in D.C. and 6 degrees in Myrtle Beach—can you believe that? Common sense demanded it to be warmer by going down South! But that wasn't the case. When I got to Myrtle Beach, which took ten hours, not my planned eight, I called my parents and gave them a hard time about not supplying me with any food or treats before I left.

Time and again, I feel the need to give my parents back some of the guilt they have riddled me with over the years. Obviously, it worked and word got around because my Grandmother sent me cookies while I was there.

For crappy hour, I went to that bar Shamrocks; we have been there together. Remember going back and forth with:

Me: "You can't beat crappy hour for this price, I'll tell you that."
You: "I wouldn't even try."
Me: "Why would you try?"
You: "You wouldn't."
Me: "You'd be crazy to try."

Janis Joplin's "Bobby McGee" was playing at the bar, "Feeling good was good enough for me," and, "freedom is just another word for nothing left to lose." Unbelievable lyrics!

First, I had the courage to have a Johnny Courage and half a dozen shrimp for two dollars. Then I tried a Rickard's Red from Molson with a half dozen plump oysters that couldn't be finer for two dollars more. You positively can't beat that for four dollars and Eric Clapton on the radio to boot, forget about it.

"I wouldn't even try."

It seems that Howard Stern has made his way down to Myrtle Beach. I'm psyched!

I didn't leave the house because of the cold; I stayed inside and forced myself to watch TV for an entire day. Here is a funny *Brady Bunch* realization: I think I figured out when Greg had sex with Florence Henderson. It was the episode when they go to the Grand Canyon. Mike had to hike 20 miles down the road to get help because Thurston Howell the Third stole their car. He told Greg to stay behind and "be the man." Well, Greg got behind all right, and he "be-da-man!"

Basically, Mike told Greg to have sex with Florence Henderson! I figure it was probably Mike's way of getting Florence Henderson off his back because Mike was gay, and he didn't want to have sex with her. Now that I think about it, I wonder why Mike didn't ask Greg to go with him???

I remembered watching The Courtship of Eddie's Father as a child and, at the time, I remembered liking it, but I think *The Courtship of Eddie's Father* was the gayest show on TV. All I'm saying is watch it as an adult in the '90s and you tell me whether I'm wrong.

Northern Exposure, however, is one of the great shows on TV. The episode where Maurice puts a Stradivarius away in a safe so no one could use it, so he could increase the value of the violin, was on. The point of the episode is a good one: If you keep something hidden and don't use that special something or share it with others, it has no meaning or value. It could be food or music or art or people. To have meaning in life, it needs to be used and shared. A Stradivarius needs to be played and listened to. The good china needs to be put out and ate from. People need to feel and be experienced.

It seems that with all my planning and packing I forgot my maps back home. I still have my plans, but I forgot the maps. I went to the store and bought a dictionary, and *A Road Less Traveled*, the first book I'll read in a long time.

"Life is a journey not a destination..."

I miss you more than I could ever tell you. I wish you were here on this trip with me.

Without you to share all this wonder with, it's hard to be complete. I try to believe you are always with me.

    I love you always,
    Nick
    -FeenX

January 1994
Washington, D.C.

Reflective Tribute
—FeenX

First Steps

Written Journal Entry
January 27, 1994
Midnight Rambles

Raped by Impatience, Aggravation, and Competence, Perseverance reluctantly gave birth to, what the world will ultimately call the Irascible Chef.

Nick Anthony is the Irascible Chef.

The concept of Irascible Chef has been in the works for many years and it is now time for him to walk the earth and change the way we cook and dine. I've decided to release some of my favorite recipes into the wild. I give you the ingredients and you figure it out! Some of recipes I've learned along the way. Some I've begged for or borrowed. Some I just outright stole. Some are manipulated classics and some are family secrets. So the recipes I release today are for all to create for themselves. The recipes I may reveal while on this journey will be known as, the Road Recipes.

Little secret: Just to let you know there are people everywhere watching, looking, and waiting for a secret to get out. Ironically, people on both sides are working equally hard to either conceal for themselves or reveal the secret out into the world. Family secrets are just that, and if everyone had the recipe, everyone could make it—diluting the value, making it less special.

As an artist, I have incorporated a philosophy with regard to the recipes I create and use. Considering the way the recipes had to be decoded and refined in the first place—a pinch of this and *two bunch* of that, required creativity, experience, and experimentation. Nothing was truly given, so nothing can be truly given away. Even some of my recipes change with the weather.

Besides, if I had a nickel for every minute I wasted giving a recipe or direction... Nobody follows directions exactly or at all anyway and sometimes adjustments need to be made on the fly. Just because you have the recipe for Coke Classic doesn't mean you can duplicate it. My reputation/life are on the line here! Do I really need someone to say I got this recipe from Nick Anthony and someone else saying—this food sucks, Nick Anthony sucks! I refuse to accept responsibility that someone given all the tools, is going to get the same results I would. I'm sorry; you're on your own here!

Some people might think this is unfriendly, unhelpful, and dare I say irascible... I look at it as encouraging creativity, giving out a piece of clay to be molded, the opportunity of creating something original and maybe even better than mine... Right.

So my philosophical irascibility stands! All you get is an ingredient list and some simple instructions—no amounts. How do I know how many people you're cooking for anyway? At least you have a chance! I'll show you the pond and the bait—you get the fish out of the goddamned water!

Road Recipe

Chicken Soup—It's soup, how hard could it be?
(Recipe from Grammy)

Ingredients:
   Chicken legs and thighs
   Carrots
   Onions
   Garlic
   Celery
   Tomato
   Water
   Salt and pepper
   Chicken bouillon
   Butter
   Parmesan

Directions:
1. Combine all ingredients and reduce by half.
2. Pull cooked chicken meat from bones and reserve
3. Hand blend reduced stock until smooth
4. Boil orzo in chicken stock cook until al dente, strain.
5. Add orzo, butter, and pulled chicken to cooked soup.
6. Serve with grated Parmesan *optional

Suggestions:
Cocktail: Whiskey sour
Wine: Something light and crisp—Sauvignon Blanc
Beer: Something dry, effervescent and light—Coors, PBR
Music: "Mambo Italiano" by Rosemary Clooney, Big Night

Chapter 5
Atlanta Brave

Audio Journal from the Car

January 28, 1994
Mood: Upbeat

11:00 a.m.

Testing, testing... I have my lucky shirt on! Actually, it's one of Richard's shirts. He unintentionally gifted it to me when I stayed at his place after a long night out. It was Richard's it had to be lucky.

Leaving Myrtle Beach, headed to Georgia, hoping not to eat a peach! Weather is cold, and the skies cloudy...

11:03 a.m.

It was a day like any other day. I left this small town for the apple in decay. It was my destiny, it's what I needed to do, they were telling me, I'm telling you. Bum-bum-bum-bum! Cool! Ha hahahaha. Foreigner's, "Long, Long, Way from Home" is being repeated on the radio.

> *"It was a Monday*
> *A day like any other day"*

See, just like I've been singing.

11:47 a.m.

I've been listening to Derek and the Dominoes, Allman Brothers. Funny, I've been talking about not eating a peach and boom—here it is! The Allman Brothers, "Sweet Melissa" is on the radio.

> *"Crossroads, seem to come and go, yeah.*
> *The gypsy flies from coast to coast*
> *To sweet Melissa... mmm..."*

Atlanta Brave—Letter 2
February 9, 1994

Hi, Laura,
 I hope you are well. These are the latest events:
 I was only able to stay at my parents' condo for a week because it was being rented out after that. Before I left Myrtle Beach, I exchanged my New York license plates for plates from South Carolina to avoid any hassles that being from New York might bring me. My next stop was Georgia, the land of peaches, hot, humid weather and some of my good old friends. I drove down to South Carolina through Charleston. Historic Charleston was still recovering from their last hurricane, I believe it was called hurricane Andrew. It was unfortunate for me because everything I wanted to take pictures of had scaffolding all over it or was esthetically damaged. I'm sure the Charlestonians didn't care much for the damage or the repair either.
 To keep me awake while driving, I practiced my harmonica and managed to get to Savannah by nightfall. Playing the harmonica is hard and I'm awful at it.
 When I got to Savannah, it was totally black. Everything was black there—the sky was black, all the people were black, and from the rain the road was shiny and black. Every street that I turned on or off seemed to be named Martin Luther King Avenue. I couldn't figure out where I was going. I was supposed to stay at a hostel downtown off Martin Luther King Avenue, but when I drove by it, I said, "NO FREAKIN' WAY!" At that point on the trip, I couldn't afford anything happening to my car or my belongings.

It looked like a demilitarized zone near the hostel and that made the decision for me. I didn't even want to get out of the car. I've only heard good things about Savannah, and I didn't see much, but I did fear for my safety the whole time I was there.

I couldn't let my imagination run me out of town like that; I had to prove that I was being ridiculous. I saw a Popeyes restaurant and knew I could get some good spicy fried chicken, beans, rice, and biscuits. And I'll tell you what—Popeyes was some damn good eats! I haven't had Popeyes in years, and it was as good as I remembered. As I sat down, I felt as though everyone were thinking, "Who does this white boy think he is eating in our restaurant?"

The entire time I was there, I didn't see one other white person and it made me quite uncomfortable. I thought I was going to die based on the fact that I was white. Being on the minority side of things does give you a different perspective. However, no one ever bothered, threatened, or harassed me. This feeling of fear was only going on in my head and it wasn't fair at all. The police did happen to be all over the place, busting people around me, for what appeared to be hanging out—Was I so naïve?

After facing a few fears and enjoying a very satisfying dinner, I decided it was okay for me to leave Savannah to the night and to drive four hours to Atlanta. It was 9 p.m. when I started out for Atlanta, and I had no idea where to go when I got there.

It took me forever to finally get to Atlanta. When I got into town, I was supposed to stay with my friend June, but she wasn't expecting me until the next day. I spent the night in a run-down motel by the side of the road because I felt a little uncomfortable calling and imposing myself on June so late at night.

Interestingly enough, back in November I saw June at a high school reunion and she told me that if I were ever in Georgia, I could stay with her and her roommate. I never would have thought that I could take her up on such an offer.

It's funny how your perspective evolves as you get older. It wasn't long ago that I would never have accepted anyone's offer to come and stay with him or her. I thought that people made these kind of offers as gestures to be nice; I never imagined taking anyone up on it.

In my mind, I thought if I accepted these offers from people, I would owe them something in return—as if that would be the worst thing in the world. I also didn't want people to think I was a moocher, or the stereotypical guest who never leaves, eats the host out of house and home, and makes a mess everywhere. It's kind of a fucked up thought process. I know, I know, after all I'm on card number one of the Topps Neurotic Card Series—Nick Anthony-in-action!

I'm trying to look at life differently. What is the point of having these great friends and family if they make offers and you don't accept them? Shouldn't you share and enjoy life together? Wherever I stayed I wanted to establish that I would never outstay my welcome, try to help out wherever I could, and to try to leave the smallest footprints possible, so that I wouldn't be a burden to anyone, including myself.

My greatest fear on this trip was that someone who had helped me out would say, "Thank

God he's gone!" I know, who would ever say that about me—right...?

When I arrived at June's condo, I stepped out of the car; it was cold and there was a relentless, miserable, misty rain coming down. It was as cold as it could be without changing the thick mist to snow. The temperature was slightly warmer than Myrtle, but it still wasn't the kind of warmer weather I was hoping for.

Ironically, the same minute that I knocked on the door, the phone rang. In the background I could hear it was Patrick, June's ex-husband. It just so happens that Patrick was also a close buddy of mine from high school. He was calling June from Chicago. June and I both laughed at the synchronicity of my arrival and Patrick's call. It later came out that for no good reason Patrick was jealous of me because June wrote my farewell blurb in our senior yearbook. I plan to stay with Patrick whenever I get to his side of the country.

I had a nice comfortable spot at June's two-bedroom apartment. The futon in the living room was just perfect. June has a roommate, Ann, and the three of us get along pretty well. The routine at June's was pretty much the same every day. While June and Ann were at work or school, I would tour in and around Atlanta.

The highway system around Atlanta is weird. Instead of having four highways going in the four directions, they have one highway that circles the entire city. So the same highway goes North, South, East, and West—depending where you are on the circle. One day I ended up going around the entire circle because when I should have gone east I went south. So instead of taking a five-minute trip, it took me an hour because I had to go all the way around the city.

One day I took the MARTA, Atlanta's public transportation system, to go to a couple of art galleries downtown. I saw my first original Ansel Adams photograph, and it was spectacular!

An observation that disturbed me happened on an escalator at the MARTA station. There was this old woman with a cane, and this man behind her was in such a rush to get by her he practically knocked her down. Meanwhile, you could see from her scattering eyes and shaky cane skills that she was nervous about riding the escalator in the first place. And, this jerk is in such a rush he can't wait two extra seconds; he practically knocked her down. I'm thinking how pissed I would be if she were my grandmother. Why have we forsaken human decency because we are in such a rush? What kind of people are we that we have lost all sense of respect for each other! We don't care about anyone else except ourselves; we are desensitized to the people around us. It's so sad; it's so scary it makes me want to holler!

Most nights, I cooked for June and Ann and we drank many bottles of wine, laughed, and talked about every subject. One night, I even gave a cooking lesson, which I always enjoy.

Every night the three new roommates had what we called "sessions." During these sessions we would debate, explore, and analyze any subject. Something in life that I truly miss is philosophy and debates—and these sessions were so refreshing and real.

In high school, we used to analyze everything and have discussions about it: politics, religion, sex, death penalty, abortion, etc. No matter what the topic, it was constructive, educational, and transcending.

I love when people are pro-choice and against the death penalty at the same time. It's usually an easy victory because their arguments usually negate themselves.

June, Ann, and I solved all the world's little problems. We argued a lot, in an intelligent way, sharing our individual views, and we really listened to what we each had to say. You know how I like a good argument. Just give me a side, I don't even have to believe in it, and ring the bell.

One of the many lessons I've learned in life is that you have to be willing to hear what other people have to say and be willing to change your views or beliefs if they're askew. When I was in high school, I had completely different views on abortion, the death penalty, gun control, and so many other topics. It's possible that over time my views could change again. With age hopefully comes wisdom and understanding. If you're not willing to make corrections to your map when it's wrong, you will always be lost.

Whenever we had a session, it seemed as though we would somehow end up talking about Patrick. We would talk a little welfare reform and end up talking a little Patrick. Talk a little disarming the government and talk a little Patrick. Abortion—Patrick. Death penalty—Patrick. Sex—Patrick. Whatever—Patrick.

There is much pain and therapy going on at June's—she's still recovering from her relatively new divorce.

June and Patrick were high school sweethearts and eventually got married after a rocky relationship after college. She is still very bitter about the reasons for the breakup and is languishing in the healing process. I listened to her side of things, and I truly felt for her. When I get to the other side of the country, I will probably get Patrick's side of things and feel for him. Who knows?

On one evening, I had a session with June alone. June had been looking very down to the point of crying. I told her it was okay to cry if she wanted to—I would be there for her. She told me that she doesn't have any more tears and something about it not being an acceptable public form of expression when she was growing up. It made me sad, and I felt helpless.

June and I got into talking about when people get married then divorced, and everyone comes running to play armchair quarterback. The professionals come out with nonsense such as:

"I tried telling you that you shouldn't get married."

"I told you that you were too young."

"I told you that you weren't right for each other, etc."

I told June, "I think their day-after analysis is a bunch of self-serving, guilt-relieving horse shit. People just don't have the guts to say what it takes at the point of confrontation. They might think it and discuss it with others, but they don't say it to the person who matters."

June asked, "Don't you think people should tell you whether they know of a reason you shouldn't get married?"

I said, "Yes, I do. You should. But listen. People, my friends, my family, all of them say they said something. They say that they told me, something like 'Are you sure you really want to go through with this?' What the fuck is that question supposed to evoke?

Granted, I was the kind of person who thought I knew everything. I probably wouldn't have let anyone tell me differently anyway, but had they said more, it might have given me something to think about. Understand, I'm not blaming anyone. Everyone has to take responsibility for his or her actions. I just feel that for someone to say something that would make a difference, you need to say something of substance that rocks their world, the kind of something that might put your relationship on the line.

I told June that most people are not willing to put an important relationship on the line. I wasn't ready to do that with my brother or Patrick or Richard. The questions you need to ask and the levels you need to reach to make a difference are very scary, unknown, and can do major damage to a relationship. The damage may be irreparable. Someday, I hope to have that kind strength, to do what it takes.

June asked me what I thought about Richard and Silvia's wedding and if I thought they could make a marriage work. I told her that if anyone seems to have a solid enough relationship, I would say they have a good shot at making it work. They have dated on and off for over ten years. They have what appears to be a very open and equal relationship, and I think equality plays a major role in success. Everyone needs their own time, space, activities, and friends. There is no room for jealousy or holding on too tightly. Richard lets her live her life, and Silvia lets him live his, and I think that can be one of the healthiest parts of a relationship.

You know, Laura, that was one thing that I certainly didn't have in my marriage, and I did have with you.

After staying with June for about two weeks, I stayed with another buddy of mine, David, who also lives in Atlanta. All the people who live there call Atlanta "Hotlanta," although, it hasn't been hot while I've been here. The weather was, however, warmer in Hotlanta than other places I've been so far on this trip.

David was another alumnus from my high school. Actually, David was in my core group of friends in the good old days, a "brethren" if you will.

David has carved out a wonderful world for himself in Atlanta—far from his family in New York. He calls himself, "The kid," pronounced the *Keed*. The Keed is a great person married to a Southern Belle, named Karen, who appears to keep him in line as his mother, "The Warden," did back in the old days. David refers to his wife, Karen, as "The Babe," pronounced "The Babe."

The Keed and The Babe have an immaculate, large, four-bedroom colonial that Karen decorated better than Martha Stewart could have ever done! Martha annoys the hell out of me! I think Martha annoys the hell out of everyone!

Karen made The Keed and me a fabulous feast of fresh tuna steaks infused with an oriental marinade, sautéed broccoli with lemon and pine nuts, and red roasted potatoes with fresh herbs. For dessert, Karen made a chocolate mousse cake with a raspberry sauce. Everything was made from scratch, and I really appreciated the effort. I love when people go the extra yard to impress my palate; the mere fact that they tried, the effort alone impresses the hell out of me. This particular effort was not only major, but happened to be delicious as well. I definitely let Karen know how good her meal was because she was a bit intimidated to be cooking for me, with my culinary background and all.

    I think it's funny that people get nervous when they're preparing food for me. I understand that they're not professionals. To tell you the truth, I wouldn't let them know whether it was terrible even if it were garbage. The ironic part is that people don't realize the tremendous amount of pressure I put on myself when I cook for them. People have higher expectations because I am a school-educated chef; it can't just be good, it has to be great—every time! If they only knew how nervous I was preparing food for them, they would laugh.

    After dinner, we talked about the June and Patrick divorce since they were all friends. Patrick is the one who introduced David to Karen. I told them there was a lot of hurting at June's house, and June's friends were feeding the manifestation beast. Her friends hated Patrick! That made it more difficult for June. June said they never saw the good side of him and that the condemnation wasn't completely fair.

    Karen and David both told me that they still liked Patrick, but they don't like what went down. I told them the same thing I told June: "There are always three sides to every story… I still like Patrick and we're friends because he is like a brother. Even if your brother does something against you or something that you don't agree with, it doesn't stop him from being your brother."

    To cap off the night on a much lighter note, we talked about my next destination. Karen gave me all kinds of places I should go when I travel to New Orleans. Karen is originally from Mobile,

Alabama and has been to New Orleans many times before. I'm psyched to be going to New Orleans and Mardi Gras! It was so great to watch Karen tell me about New Orleans. Karen's eyes lit up; she was so full of enthusiasm—it reminded me so much of you, Laura. You would like David and Karen.

Who would have thought I would be going to all these great places????!!!!

David travels a lot for work, and he asked me whether I would like to go on the road with him. Of course, I jumped at the opportunity and went along for the ride for a couple of days. We went to Knoxville, Tennessee and stayed at a hotel in Cedar Bluff. Once again, I was riding for free on the hospitality of another corporate sponsor; it was David's company's turn this time. David's job was much more grown up than the summer job he had back in high school at the Montauk A&P grocery store. I remember going to Montauk for summer family vacations and running into him at the grocery store, and he was instructing other employees what to do while he was dressed in a button-down shirt with a tie and shorts—it was a sight!

The next day we went to Chattanooga, Tennessee and I saw the Chattanooga Choo-Choo!!! When we traveled through these towns, it seemed as though we were transported back through time. It was like the towns were frozen in the 1950s. The buildings and fixtures were all old but looked new. The people were all wearing old-style clothes, milling around, but not really going anywhere, seemingly with no purpose. I felt as though I were in a "Twilight Zone" episode.

The two of us drove though the Smoky Mountains, which did appear to be mountains smoldering after a fire. They look like ripples of mountain ranges, each one lying against the next, in a smoky haze. The Smoky Mountains were my first National Park on my list of parks to see. Unfortunately, the weather prevented us from seeing too much of them.

While David was in meetings all day, I stopped by some brewpub in Chattanooga called Big River. I didn't think they would have a brewpub in this remote area, but they did, and they made some damn good beer to boot. I also went to the aquarium while in Chattanooga. When I think about an aquarium, I think of a place that has all kinds of sea world stuff, including sharks and whales. My perception of the world revolves around the North East type of thinking. The aquarium had only river life indigenous to the Tennessee River, which makes sense since this aquarium was on the Tennessee River.

This trip is a big learning experience, opening my eyes to many wonderful things. We finished our mini-trip at Stone Mountain back in Atlanta where Stonewall Jackson is carved on this huge granite mountain. You can see all of downtown Atlanta from the top. I took a gondola ride the entire way up. I believe Stonewall watched Atlanta burn from the top of this mountain during the Civil War.

It was great reliving the old times with David; we just picked up where we left off some ten years ago as if no time went by at all. He welcomed me into his home like a brother and offered me a place to stay anytime I was in town. David is a solid friend and a good man.

Unfortunately, I have to leave Hotlanta sooner than I want to. It seems I screwed up my timing for Mardi Gras. I thought that Mardi Gras started on Fat Tuesday, but actually Fat Tuesday is the end of the celebration. Fat Tuesday is the last celebration before Ash Wednesday, which kicks off the Lenten season and formally starts the sacrifice that ends the Mardi Gras. Now that it has been explained to me, it all makes sense.

    I'm so grateful to have such great friends. It made me realize that life is about so much more than what we all think it is about. I guess we should say a sarcastic "thanks" to the society at large that leads us to believe that life is about how hard you work and how much money you have versus the value of sharing quality time with family and friends. The value of health, happiness, and love are also secondary in our screwed up world!

    It is sad leaving June and David. I do think my stay worked out better than anyone expected. And it also renewed friendships that will, hopefully, last a lifetime. Of course, the storm of 1994 is forecasted for the area I am traveling through, as I leave Georgia.

    I hope you got the picture I sent from D.C. If you did, I'm sure you can't see how cold it is. I miss you to the point of pain. Tom Petty says, "The *waiting* is the hardest part," but if you don't know what you're waiting for how can it be?

    The cows are not coming home!

    I *love* you and miss you very much. I wish you were here!

        I love you,

        Nick
        -FeenX

January 1994
Antebellum, Georgia

Tea for Two

—FeenX

Road Recipe

Filet Mignon au Poivre — I see you're feeling lucky!
(My version of a classic!)

Ingredients / Beef:
- Filet mignon
- Butter
- Onion powder
- Rosemary olive oil
- Rough cracked black pepper and kosher salt

Ingredients / Sauce:
- Beef demi-glace
- Cognac
- Rough cracked black pepper
- Butter
- Heavy cream
- Shallots
- Rosemary oil

Directions:
1. **Season and Marinate:** filet mignon with onion powder, rosemary oil, rough cracked black pepper, and kosher salt.
2. **Sauté:** Seasoned filet in hot butter.
3. **Sauce:** Sauté butter, heavy cream, onion powder, rosemary oil, rough cracked black pepper, beef demi glace, cognac — ignite and reduce by 2/3rds.
4. **Serve** sauce over filet garnish with fresh rosemary and rough cracked black pepper.

Suggestions:
- **Cocktail:** Skyy vodka on the rocks with a lime
- **Wine:** Full-bodied — Cabernet Sauvignon
- **Beer:** Black and Tan — Guinness & Bass
- **Music:** "Fly Me to the Moon" by Frank Sinatra

Chapter 6

Leavin' Leesiana

Audio Journal from the Car

February 10, 1994
Mood: Ambivalent

11:00 a.m.
Testing, testing… I'm leaving Georgia today, it's kind of cold, 30 degrees, pissy rain, but I have my lucky shirt on and, once again, I'm on the road with my best face forward.

Pearl Jam's "Alive" is on the radio.

"I, oh, I'm still alive
Hey I, oh, I'm still alive"

11:03 a.m.
Staying with June and Ann reminded me of Bevis and Butthead, only because of their brown and blonde hair color …actually, staying with them was more like "Three's Company." I was Jack, and they played Chrissy and Janet—ahahahahah! And, June, guess who you get to be—not-so-dumb-blonde, what do you think about that, Chrissy? Ahhh, huh, huhuhuhh.

Talked to Laura before I left and there wasn't a whole lot of talking, which kind of makes me sad… But, I'm gonna try to take Mina's advice, not take it personally, and hope everything works out.

Feeling anxious, a little nervous—first time I'm headed into uncharted waters. My father called me to tell me about a major blizzard hitting N.Y. and that I was headed into a monsoon. Typhoon, tornadoes, wrath of God shit! But, I was watching the weather channel and didn't see any of what they were talking about. Well, I'm on my way, I guess the worst thing I could do is pull over—wouldn't be the end of the world...

12:15 p.m.

Beep Beep... Beep Beep...Beep Beep. Uh, up, up, up, there's the beeper, the beeper is going off, Its Uncle Charlie and Camilla. Psych! I was just thinking about them. I'm glad they called and they used my codes. Can't pull over right now. Finally, someone's using codes. 511 means, calling to say hi, call back.

Well, you certainly don't see that every day—Strange plant life here called "kudzu"—a vine from Japan that was supposed to control land erosion and has done nothing but kill other foliage, taking over like Godzilla.

Flashing lights! Bright lights! Whizzing up behind me and flying past me! FUCK! My heart is in my throat! I thought I was getting pulled over, but the cop blew right by me to catch someone else.

Madonna's "Into the Groove" is on the radio.

"And you can dance
For inspiration"

My new beeper message for the new leg of my trip: Life is a journey, not a destination. I'm headed to New Orleans. Leave your message at the beep...

12:46 p.m.
There is something going on with the left side of my nose. I just keep pulling more and more crap out of it and it seems to be never ending. It's disgusting. Yuck…

My speedometer stopped working the moment I left Georgia, but at least the odometer is still working. So by tracking and timing the mile markers, it looks like I'm doing fifty-second miles. I have to figure out how fast that is—flat road, fifth gear, 3,300 rpm…

So far, I don't know what my parents are talking about; the weather is fine. Every time I hear the weather report on the radio, they say nothing about bad weather where I am or where I am going. They mention the blizzard up north, but nothing here. I mean I hope it doesn't get bad.

Now I'm going 3,500 rpm and 46-second miles…

1:00 p.m.
The Chattahoochee is everywhere and I'm 100 miles out of Atlanta. Just entered Alabama! Welcome to Alabama the Beautiful! Governor Jim Folsom. Another state checked off the list…

Outlaw Josie Wales! The Rose of Alabamee!

Sam Bottoms: "You know the Rose of Alabama, Jesse?"

Clint Eastwood: "I reckon not."

I wonder if I'm driving by the stadium at Auburn Hills...

I just entered Macon County and kudzu is crawling all over Alabama.

Ever since I've driven through Montgomery everyone seems to be driving like assholes! I'm headed for a-Mobile, Alabama!

Ughh! A stinking bus just cut me off! It's starting to suck not having a speedometer and having to rely on the tach for my speed.
"I will endeavor to persevere"—Also from Outlaw Josie Wales.
I better not slow down or this kudzu will crawl all over me.
I just saw my first Alabama cop—just a regular cop with regular lights, making it easy to distinguish from the other cars…
2:00 p.m.
I need to start having my cameras here by my side while I'm driving so if something spontaneous happens I can shoot away. Like, I just passed this tractor-trailer that has just flipped over and is all over the road. It would have made a cool picture.
The kudzu is growing so fast I can actually see it moving! The kudzu is alive, green, and taking over the planet! Observation about the water down here: it's all muddy brown. Maybe that's why they call it Muddy Water. I don't know.
I'm almost in Mobile and I'm pumped!
You should see all the hicks driving around in fucking pickup trucks without a clue about what this country is, I don't know, all about. Maybe they do know and it's me who's clueless.

4 Non Blondes "What's Up" is on the radio.

> *"And so I wake in the morning*
> *And I step outside*
> *And I take a deep breath and I get real high"*

I'm so unable to hit the high notes of this damn song.
"This country is just one giant pussy just waiting to get fucked!" —Tony Montana

While driving along I realize that I'm the only one driving in a stinking car alone—everyone else is traveling with others—but that's not a problem...

BAM! Oh! Somebody is getting tagged, I don't know but my heart is still fucking pumping as the trooper just blew by me. Wow, that was close.

Tip: Slam on the brakes even if the cop sees you—it will make a difference when they hit you with the radar... Oh, oh, I just got a beep from Charlie and Camilla again!

Lynyrd Skynyrd, "What's Your Name" is on the radio.

> *"What's your name, little girl?*
> *What's your name?*
> *Shootin' you straight, little girl?*
> *Won't you do the same?"*

Poor little German Shepherd doggie wandering on the side of the road, lost. Probably going to be dead in a second...

Beep, beep... Oh, they're beeping me again. Goddamn it, I don't know what to do. I'm on the road, the road to nowhere.

Counting Crows "Mr. Jones" is on the radio.

> *"Mr. Jones and me tell each other fairy tales*
> *Stare at the beautiful women*
> *"She's looking at you. Ah, no, no, she's looking at me."*

First things first, I need to get to New Orleans, find the campground, get set up, and then I will call Uncle Charlie...

Okay, okay, now I'm getting somewhere—welcome to Mississippi, baby! It's amazing how everything's not like a dense forest, but sparse and 3-D-like...

M—I—S—S—I—S—S—I—P—P—I !

5:00 p.m.
Gotta tell you, man, everyone looks like they're ready to party, party, party! I'll tell you that! You think they're going to Mardi Gras?

Troopers are everywhere!

Everyone everywhere is putting their party hats on. I can feel it, they're pumped for me, and I'm pumped for me! I'm going it alone, but I'm still psyched!

There is a lot of cool scenery down here. We certainly live in a beautiful country! I'm definitely not dressed right for this weather. I'm fucking hot already! Left rainy, drizzly, disgusting, 30-degree weather, and now it's 70 degrees at 5:20 p.m.

Cool thing about the highway system down South. They have these cool bumps in the road, so if you drift off, the bumps snap you out of it. I don't understand why you couldn't do that up North—all these excellent ideas. I just don't know…

Just passed a sign: New Orleans 97 miles away, 5:30 now, about two hours, should be there by 7:30 or so. The sun should still be way out—I hope. I should be fine…

I think there's gambling in Mississippi. There are a lot of gambling places—cool! Biloxi, Mississippi is 13 miles away but it's not like Africa hot or nothing. So it's okay…

Now entering Biloxi! Now entering Biloxi!

I just saw what appears to be a typical Biloxi, Mississippi family in a big Ford pickup truck—mother, father, two or three kids—all in the front seat, lovin' life.

This audio journal will be great to have and hear someday! I'll be able to feel my mood at that splinter in time instead of trying to remember the feeling when I'm writing it down in my journal!

I wonder if Laura gets angry thinking that I'm off traveling, seeing the country, doing what I'm doing. I wonder if she thinks I'm off having a party… I wonder what she thinks.

Allman Brothers "Ramblin' Man" is on the radio.

> *"Lord, I was born a ramblin' man…"*
> *"Tryin' to make a livin' and doin' the best I can…"*

Howard Stern's on out here, too! I've always wanted to go to Mardi Gras. Who would have thought I'd be going at this stage of my life, by myself, and sleeping in a tent?

My back is starting to bother me, the sun is going down, I just want to get my tent set up and go out on this town. I just entered Louisiana! Yahoo! Went through a lot of states today. I didn't realize there was such a long bridge to get into New Orleans. We have a beautiful sunset going on.

Bonnie Tyler "Total Eclipse of the Heart" is on the radio.

> *"Once upon a time I was falling in love*
> *But now I'm only falling apart*
> *There's nothing I can do"*

It just occurred to me, David told me I would gain an hour by crossing time zones. I just gained an hour! Not going to help with the sunlight to set up my tent though. On the radio they're talking about the traffic that I'm sitting in.

I need to get some pictures of the New Orleans skyline. Nice sunset.

They just said there is no parking in the French Quarter and if you get in an accident, hold off till Wednesday to report it. Nice!

I hope I have a cool spot at the campground. It's starting to get dark… I need to call Uncle Charlie.

9:00 p.m.

I just set up the tent—no problems, it took forever. I felt like everyone was watching me. I have to get over that issue of mine. Very cool place, cool everything. It was dark during the whole setup process and I still did it. Time to go into the Quarter and find a phone!

✦ ✯ ✸

February 12, 1994

Mood: Excited

They pour grain alcohol straight from the bottle here. I had fried alligator last night—my diet has been horrendous lately, fried food on top of fried food, Popeyes on top of Popeyes on top of Popeyes.

A sign in the window at Nick's in Metairie, "All women who don't wear underwear —Drink free all night long" —what planet am I on? Ohh! Maybe I could be the guy who checks!

Derek and the Dominoes "Layla" is on the radio.

> "…you got me on my knees
> Layla, I'm begging darling, please"

This New Orleans is one of the most unbelievable places. I could definitely see myself living here for part of the year.

An idea just came to me: I could set up a studio with pictures of New Orleans… "Nawlins!"

Sorry, about that, it's not "New Orleeeeeens" it's respectfully and affectionately pronounced "Nawlins."

    I went to this gallery, and they were charging like $15,000 for Ansel Adams prints. The prints were in a gallery off of Royale Street. Maybe I could charge individuals out the ass for my photo services.

    I miss Laura a lot… Makes me. Very. Sad…

Written Journal Entry

February 18, 1994

Incense and Crystals

 I went to a tarot reader today. I know, you're asking me, what am I doing going to a card reader? Well, it's a little-known family secret that we consort with psychics. I know what you're thinking, but speaking with psychics isn't reserved only for desperate and hopeless people—kings, queens, and presidents have sought their services. For as long as I can remember, we've had a family psychic. Yes, family psychic not a family psychiatrist, although we should have had one of them too. It's always been someone in the family or someone very close to the family. It's someone we've looked to over the years for guidance during trying times: times of family illness, times of problems within a marriage, times of extended unemployment or money shortages, and times of great unhappiness. As the Monkees used to sing, "I'm a believer." I'm not saying that I believe all psychics are clairvoyant. I'm saying that psychics aren't necessarily charlatans. Some people are truly gifted with ultra-intuitiveness and have the *shine*. The family psychics that we have sought insight from have been on target almost 99 percent of the time. Personally, I choose not to live and die according to the insights provided, but I do listen and take it for what it is—a guide.

 If you still think I'm crazy, there was a time when the police even took a chance on our psychic to help find a missing child. The child had been missing without any clues for some months. As it turned out, the psychic pointed the police to the icy waters below an old rickety dock in the dead of winter in Long Island. The police pulled out the child's lifeless body exactly where she told them it would be. I've never had my cards read directly, but I did listen to the advice and heed their warnings given to me by my mother. Infidelities, times of death, good times ahead, and also choices that could prevent tragedy, have all been predicted. Events can be changed in some instances. Because we have choices in life, we can choose to go down many paths that all create new and different choices that can change the outcome of our existence. One choice could set in motion a change in your final destiny.

I chose to go to this psychic partially to see what would be predicted, cat killing curiosity, and finally because I was in *Nawlins*. However, I was taking a big chance by going to an unknown card reader. I was a bit hesitant because in the past, I've always known the source, and have had the safety of a buffer—my mother.

I'm only going to mention this little nugget. The old crystal ball gazing woman had all the accoutrements including a physical description to beat the band—portly, wrinkled, with an assortment of varying colored warts and moles (with and without hair) on her face. (Of course she did…)

She predicted, "An awakening from denial is a slow, but necessary process."

If you want to know any more detail may I suggest you go to your own psychic?

I'm sorry, but what good would telling you any more information be any way? An awakening from denial is a slow, but necessary process—what the hell is that supposed to mean?

Leavin' Leesiana—Letter 3
February 21, 1994

Hi, Laura,

I've been thinking about you, and I hope this letter finds you well.

I'm sadly about to leave New Orleans. And as I'm a newly proclaimed southerner I pronounce it like a native —Nawlins. I must say un-fucking-believable! There was a possibility that some of my friends would join me in New Orleans for the celebration, but those plans fell through for one reason or another. So, I forced myself to overcome and conquer it alone. Can somebody please twist my arm? Actually, I did have some anxiety because it was a little intimidating camping, partying, meeting people, and dining out by myself, but you can't let your fear limit your existence. My heart tells me that I definitely have to live in New Orleans for part of the year. The "laissez-faire" attitude is the right attitude—the only tude to have. The music comes out of the walls!

- Oh, the Jazz and blues…!
- The food is amazing…!
- The people—all very colorful…!
- The partying—that never ends…!
- The drinks—don't let me forget the drinks…!

In New Orleans, you can drive up to the drive-through window at a frozen daiquiri place and get a frosty, freezy daiquiri with 190-proof grain alcohol and a straw to enjoy while you're cruising down the street. Now mind you, I'm not recommending this to amateurs, but, if you are a professional, I highly recommend it.

I was going down Bourbon Street, running tabs at as many bars as I could stumble in and out of. I could bring my drink from the last bar with me because each bar supplies you with to-go cups. How great is that?! I love drinking in the streets! Don't even get me going on how fabulous the café au laits and beignets are.

Let me start off by saying: I was lucky enough to get a campsite that wasn't that far away from the French Quarter. Please don't laugh, I was lucky to get a campsite, and it was only because there was a cancellation. Can you imagine that a Campground of America was the only place available in the entire city for me to sleep? The site wasn't even cheap, and, for $36 dollars a day, I had to sleep outside in my own tent. The COA did have clean bathrooms with hot showers, and they had security, so at least I felt safe. My site also had a picnic table with electric and water hookups. It was late when I first arrived at the campsite, but I still had to pitch my tent in the total darkness of a moonless night. Somehow, I did manage—I practiced setting the tent up inside my parents' condo a couple of times, but with the lights on, not in the dark.

The following day at the campsite, I met these crazy old spinsters who offered to show me around. The Golden Girls had to be anywhere in their late 50s to late 70s and they drove a camper all the way from West Virginia, to be at Mardi Gras. Johnny was the mother and leader of their gang, Ruth was Johnny's daughter, Helen was Johnny's sister, and Bobby was Helen's daughter. They were my training wheels for the first part of the day, and they really helped me get acclimated to my new surroundings. They showed me the way to get in and out of the French Quarter as well as the ins and outs of the parades. Unfortunately, kids grow up—I took the training wheels off to fly on my own to find some kids my own age for the second part of the day.

    Each day, I would get up early and take a shuttle bus into the French Quarter for a buck twenty-five. I'd return to my tent around five or six in the morning. Roosters actually crowed, which was only cool the first time! I'd crawl into my tent to sleep for a couple of hours so that I could be back on the bus by 10 a.m. headed right back to the French Quarter festivities.

    I wished so much you could've been there with me. You would have loved it! The only way it could have been better was if I had someone to share it with.

    I turned twenty-nine while I was in the Big Easy. Almost everyone found a way to get a hold of me to wish me happy birthday; somehow, the day of my birthday was a little lackluster.

    Tradition is very important to the participants and celebrants of Mardi Gras. One tradition of the Mardi Gras festivities involves organized parades with "Krewes." Krewes are men and women disguised in costumes, riding on parade floats throwing trinkets and beads, called, strangely enough, "throws" to the crowd. The amazing part of the ritual was what people were willing to do for these "throws." The ritual of girls taking their tops off for 25 cents worth of Mardi Gras plastic made me laugh; you would think they were throwing gold the way the girls rushed to get their tops off. Guys pulled down their pants to get girls to take off their tops. I guess the nonstop drinking has something to do with it. It was sheer pandemonium! I'm sure their parents must be so proud. Their parents probably did the same things! Actually, by the age of some of these people participating looks like they're still doing them!

Anything goes at the Mardi Gras! "I told the Padre, I like it here! The only thing you have to worry about is passing out and when that happens you won't know it anyway, so there is always next year?" No one is uptight; no one bothers you. It's like the "red hour" from Star Trek: No Rules!

Well, actually there are a couple of simple rules: There are things you must do at Mardi Gras and there are things you must not do—please do not confuse the two:

- You *must* plan at least thirty-five to forty minutes in advance to find a bathroom to go to or you could have an accident. It appeared that for some people to avoid the "accident," garbage pails, the floor, and even sinks are fair game for receiving urine.
- You *must not* stand behind crazy mothers and screaming children at the parades—believe me, they will kick your ass, mentally and physically.
- You *must* start looking for a $30 taxicab two hours before you want to go home if you miss the last, buck-twenty-five shuttle bus back at 12 a.m. Somehow, I managed to miss every buck-twenty-five shuttle back to my tent home. It will take you at least two hours to get the privilege of paying $30 to some scary redneck cabbie, not knowing whether he's going to kill you at his house or at the swamp, just so you could crawl into your tent.
- You *must not* look like a tourist.
- You *must* find a safe place for money and cards.

- You *must not* stand in front of someone really tall at the parade because you won't get any "throws."
- You *must* find another drink before you are finished with the drink you have, or you'll go thirsty! —A Mardi Gras Mortal Sin.
- You *must not* try to cross the parade line as a short cut to get to the other side of the street, especially at night. If you do— DO NOT, I repeat DO NOT, resist arrest. Or there is no doubt you'll be incarcerated.

If you do resist, the police WILL BEAT YOU! Deservedly so, I saw it happen. They will hogtie you and leave you like that in the middle of street while thousands of laughing onlookers taunt you, until they haul your sorry ass to jail. The police will make an example of you! If you do go to jail, do NOT, I repeat, do not pick up the soap!

My favorite bar on Bourbon Street was Port Orleans. People called me by name, when I walked inside, after only a couple of days. If I had to go to the bathroom, I went to Port Orleans— no line. If I didn't want to wait in line for a drink, I went to Port Orleans—no wait. If I didn't want to carry my camera bag any longer, I could leave it at Port Orleans—no carry.

My beers of choice were Blackened Voodoo, Dixieland Ale, or Altbeir, made in Louisiana. I saw Stephen Stills, the junior Harry Connick, Van Damme, the Neville Brothers, and Corbin Bernsen on parade floats. I ate fried alligator—a little tougher than I had hoped for. I drank Hurricanes, a sickly sweet drink with a punch invented in New Orleans at Pat O'Brien's. I went to the House of Blues, a new-concept bar fashioned after the *Blues Brothers* movie. I think Dan Aykroyd owns a piece of it. The Blues Brothers' car was even parked outside. I went to Tou-Can-Doo, a Stephen Stills, from Leesianna, bar. I went to the Crescent City Brewery and had some Crescent City beer and oysters—deeelicious!

I went to that place that David's wife, Karen, recommended, Cafe du Monde, a coffee house that is another staple in the French Quarter. For $1.98, they served you a café au lait, which is basically strong coffee with a lot of steamed milk, and three huge beignets, which are fried dough balls with enough powdered sugar to choke a horse. They would have made my grandmother and Aunt Lilly proud!

At the cemetery in New Orleans, they bury everyone in tombs above the ground. In the old days, when they buried the dead underground, they had such a problem with flooding that the coffins would float back up to the surface. It's quite a spectacle to see endless lines of tombs above ground instead of head stones. Everyone warns you to avoid the cemetery because there is a lot of crime there.

Howard Stern is on the radio in New Orleans—he's everywhere!

I tried my luck on a riverboat casino. No gambling until you pull away from the pier, of course. I got lucky and won $280 for my troubles, playing roulette! The lucky part was that I walked away while I was still up. This town has every vice you can think of; it's great!

New Orleans has everything!

As it turns out, I did have one connection in town after all—my mother's boss, Jeffrey. He was visiting exclusively for Mardi Gras, but he's originally from New Orleans, and he comes back for the festivities every year. Jeffrey says no two years are ever the same at Mardi Gras.

I ended up hanging out with Jeffrey on my birthday and on Fat Tuesday. He was a shining light that came out of nowhere. On my birthday, he picked me up at my tent and took me out for dinner to a very fine restaurant. It was nice to spend my birthday with someone I knew.

One of the highlights of Mardi Gras came on the last day. Jeffrey and I started Fat Tuesday off by stopping at this private party to get stamped so we could get back in later without any hassles. Jeffrey was able to get us into this private party that was at the Acme Oyster House. The Acme Oyster House is a famous, must-go-to staple in the French Quarter. Then we hooked up with some of Jeffrey's friends and went to the gay parade down at the end of Bourbon Street. I have never seen so many wonderfully ornate, well-put together, outrageous costumes. I also got quite an education in bondage-ware, body ornaments, tools, utensils and props! Time, effort, and energy all made for a truly amazing costume party to top all costume parties! This wasn't amateur hour! Everyone was having so much fun; wait till you see the pictures. I highly recommend going to a gay parade. Check your inhibitions at the door! You will see and experience things you could never imagine. It's certainly not the Macy's Thanksgiving Day parade I'll tell you that—much more fun!

I didn't realize at the time how lucky I was to get stamped at the Oyster House and, thank God, because Jeffrey and I ended up getting separated and lost in the wall-to-wall sea of people. There were a lot of people on Bourbon Street leading up to Fat Tuesday but nothing like the mobs of people on Fat Tuesday.

Every day, the streets got a little dirtier, and by the last and final day of the festival, I was actually walking on piles of garbage.

It started to rain, which sucked! I was lost, which sucked! I was by myself, which sucked! I had to go to the bathroom, which sucked the most!

Then, I remembered I had a safe haven to go back to. The *coup de grâce* was that it was all free—the food, the drinks, the oysters, the drinks and a bathroom—ah...There was also the possibility that Jeffrey might end up back at the Acme Oyster House, so what else could you ask for?

Jeffrey never did turn up at the Acme Oyster House, but I did meet a bunch of fun people. One older woman, in her late 50s, was trying to pick me up; I think she was anyway. She proved harmless, however, and did show me how you eat oysters in New Orleans. Belly touching the bar, beer in a frosty mug, lots of cocktail sauce, lots of Tabasco, lots of horseradish, lots of lemon, and keep them coming! They were the best oysters that I've ever had. My mouth is watering just thinking about it.

On Fat Tuesday, I ate so many oysters, or as they say in *Nawlins* "Cajun caviar," I couldn't eat no mo. Another New Orleans treat is what they call a "po boy" sandwich, and you surely haven't lived until you've eaten a po boy.

Outside my little oasis, there were so many people that you couldn't even move on the streets. If you were outside in the sea of people, you went in whatever direction the waves carried you—literally! Moving like that is a strange yet scary sensation. People were passed out like the garbage—everywhere. It was a sight!

The last night of the festival ends at 11:59:59 p.m. The police on horses come through and kick everyone off the streets, and then the street cleaners come by and clean up the rest of the mess including anyone the police missed. Just as there is zero tolerance for crossing the parade line there is zero tolerance for any disobedience at 12:00 a.m. on Ash Wednesday.

Mardi Gras is officially OVER!

Ah, CARNIVAL! Farewell to Flesh for another year!

I gave myself the treat of staying in a hotel for a couple of relaxing days after Mardi Gras was over to see what New Orleans was like after the festival. It also gave me a chance to get some more pictures of places I might have missed.

I surely couldn't leave without having another café au lait and more beignets. New Orleans is Party Central; there is never any downtime. When one festival is over, the city gears up for the next one to begin. Jazz Fest is around the corner in April, and I heard they have a "freakfest" for Halloween.

While I was lying in bed in my cozy hotel room, I got a call from Carl, one of my brother's friends. You remember Carl from the Eric Clapton concert at Brendan Byrne Arena? It was bizarre how Carl tracked me down to the hotel I was in.

Carl will be in Dallas on business, and he offered to let me stay with him at the Ritz Carlton while he's in town. I can't pass up some civilized comforts after spending a week and a half living in a tent—and it's for free! It appears as though I have another corporate sponsor! And a new destination.

Unfortunately, I have to say a sad and reluctant farewell to my latest, greatest hometown. "I will miss you, *Nawlins*, but I will be back!"

Someday, I need to bring you to New Orleans, Laura; you will love it.

"Life moves pretty fast, if you don't stop and take a look once in a while, you could miss it." —*Ferris Bueller*

      You're in my heart and soul.
      I love you very much,
      Nick
      -FeenX

February 1994
Jackson Square, N.O.

The Band

—FeenX

Road Recipe

Bananas Foster—Do this one right and you will be denied NOTHING...
(Jonathan's Bridge View restaurant in Queens—long time closed)

Ingredients:
  Ripe bananas
  Butter
  Brown sugar
  Orange and lemon zest
  Salt
  Dark rum
  Triple sec
  Banana liquor

Directions:
1. Sauté: butter, bananas, orange and lemon zest, brown sugar, salt, dark rum, triple sec, and banana liquor, ignite and reduce by 1/3.
2. Serve over Häagen-Dazs Vanilla Swiss Almond.

Suggestions:
Cocktail: Vodka Frangelico shooter, B&B, cognac
Wine: Dessert wine, tawny port, BV Muscadet
Beer: New Castle Brown Ale
Music: "It Was a Very Good Year" by Frank Sinatra or something jazzy **

Chapter 7

Deep in the Heart of Texas

Audio Journal from the Car

February 22, 1994
Mood: Laissez-faire

11:30 a.m.
I was just thinking about my next major stop—maybe, finally the Grand Canyon. That was both of our dreams, the Grand Canyon, not just mine and now I'm going to see it without her and it makes me very upset…
Pearl Jam's "Daughter" is on the radio.

"Alone…listless…breakfast table in an otherwise empty room"

Breakfast table in an otherwise empty room now it will remind me, don't call me…

11:48 a.m.
Funny, I'm driving out of "Leesiana" right now, but I'm eating McDonald's and I'm eating the French fries at the bottom of the bag. Which reminds me of the days when McDonald's was it to us kids! We all loved Mickey-D's, and eating those last French fries from the bottom of the bag was the biggest score. As kids, my brother John and I played this game where we would both grab an opposite end of the same French fry and pull it apart and whoever ended up with the longer piece was the winner, but we were

both winners because we were both eating the stinking French fries.
    U2 "Love is a Temple" is on the radio.

    "One love"

    But I remember originally coming up with this idea because I was out of French fries and I wanted MORE! We always used John's French fries. I remember, you know, that he would, after a while, initiate doing it and I remember feeling guilty because the reason I was doing it was because I wanted more French fries, and the reason he was doing it was because he was having fun playing—with his big brother! Ha! Some big brother...
    BANG, there's another cop. So far, this road has been crawling with "Copolas!" It's scaring me. So far today it seems like a nice cruising day. It's overcast, there are some dark clouds but blue skies to one side. It's cool enough I can drive with just the sun roof open, which makes for a much nicer ride...
    "Take time with a wounded hand... I'm half the man I used to be..." *singing along* Stone Temple Pilots "Creep" is on the radio.

    "Forward yesterday
    Take time with a wounded hand
    'Cause it likes to heal"

3:30 p.m.
I've just seen the coolest thing I have ever seen. There has to be at least fifty, fifty at least, like, hawks flying in a group. I've never seen anything like that. It's the wildest thing. They are just gliding along...
    Before I forget, I want to mention how many people were into the grunge scene in New Orleans. It was amazing that they would stand out, but

there were that many scattered about, to be noticed in a crowd...
3:45 p.m.
Couple experiments with photography. Trying to create a blurring effect with people in a scene. I want everything else clear; I want people to just be a blur as they are in life. It depends how steady I can hold the camera—my hands are pretty steady.

A couple of new words out of New Orleans: a *spillway* is like puddles here and there that are always there, like a river, but it's not. A stream, but it's not; it's a spillway. Just water dotted here or there. And, a line from the movie last night *The Big Easy*, I think. "You're making my tits heavy," which I equated to...

Tape ends abruptly

New tape begins

Fuck! I've been rambling on for quite a while! How long ago do you think the tape ran out, what dialog did I miss? Fuck!

Rolling Stones "Paint It Black" is on the radio.

> "No colors anymore I want them to turn black
> I see the girls walk by dressed in their summer clothes
> I have to turn my head until my darkness goes
> Hmm, hmm, hmm..."

Just cruising on highway 49 at 3,500 rpm. I don't know what the hell that means to me. I figure it's 65-70 mph—I'm not sure. And I saw the cop, thank God, I started to slow down, the second that happened the fucking radar hit me—Richard's radar detector told me. I stepped on the brake again and he drove right by! Saved again! Thank you, Richard. I mean these cops are cruising on the other side, monitoring this side—you don't see a cop on this side. You're coming the other way and it's too late. And it's all, instant on radar; cops don't cruise with it on.

Robert Cray "Smoking Gun" is on the radio.

> *"I get a constant busy signal*
> *When I call you on the phone*
> *And I know just where to find you with"*

4:10 p.m.
I'm starting to hit bugs on the windows and I don't like that one bit.

Funny, the littlest things you learn from some people. I saw this big bunch of green things scattered up in the trees. When I met the four-lady gang from West Virginia they told me it was mistletoe—interesting, it stands out as the only thing green at all.

4:45 p.m.
I had to stop to put on my Sears brand black-back-support-belt! My back was on fire!

Some drinks I've tried: Zima, kind of fruity, lemony, limey-tasting beer I don't care for too much. I definitely didn't like the Hurricane. Very sickly sweet even though supposedly it has tons of alcohol in it. What else… Something else I did care for. Um, Oh! I did like Altbier. Altbier is from a Louisiana brewery and is very good.

I just realized why it seems like I have been doing poorly on gas mileage—I've had the Mo-Fo, good-for-nothing, stinking, air-conditioner on! Goddamn it!

Extreme "More than Words" is on the radio.

"More than words..."

7:00 p.m.

Today I'm averaging 47-second miles. I still need to figure out what a 47-second mile means.

I've just searched four stations since I've crossed into Texas and every single one has been country music. I'm going to go nuts!

The sunset I'm seeing right now through Texas is unbelievable. I can't see the sun itself but the color that it's turning the sky is unbelievable. Oranges, purples, and pinks, dark blue on the outside, yellows, the clouds breaking up the colors—really cool.

Next stop: Abilene!

Deep in the Heart of Texas—Letter 4
February 26, 1994

Hi, Laura,

I hope you are receiving the letters and pictures I've been sending, and I hope you're well.

Also, I want you to know that you can call me anytime day or night. Call me if you want to talk or if you just want someone to be on the other end of the phone, I'll be there for you. You have my beeper number so it doesn't really matter where I am. Don't be afraid. Believe me—I am your friend.

I saw the most amazing sunset on the way to Dallas. Color-stained clouds littered the whole sky with deep purples, burnt oranges, piercing blues, and Crayola yellows.

Can you guess what kind of music every radio station played immediately after I crossed the border into Texas? You guessed it, country! I'm not talking most stations; I'm talking every radio station; even when I put one of my rock tapes in the player, country music came out of the speakers!

Carl and I stayed at the Ritz Carlton in downtown Dallas, and it was the cat's ass! I did the exploration thing while Carl was working at his convention. I think you would like the WestEnd Marketplace in downtown Dallas. It was the only happening spot I could find. Hip attitude, with many restaurants and shops. I ate at this place called Good Eats, and they were good eats! I had some bock beer from a local Dallas brewery; it was dark but not too bitter. I tried to get into Landry's, as in the football coach Tom Landry's restaurant, but some homeless man hounded me for money. When I told him, "no," he

Deep in the Heart of Texas

didn't accept "no," for an answer. I made the irrational mistake of pointing to my car and saying, "It just so happens that I'm currently living out of my car, so I'm homeless, too!" My paranoia wouldn't allow me to leave my car and this man together unsupervised, so I left.

Jack called to fill me in on the goings on back home. Paul left on his own sojourn, to find riches in Africa??? He had his own motivation, but everything is relative, and riches are riches; it just depends on whose scale you're using to weigh them with.

To find extra riches, Richard went to Atlantic City, with Father Moraliti, a priest from high school he was still oddly a friend with. Richard won eight grand to add to the fifteen grand he had already won for the year. Richard has always been the luckiest person on the planet. I did have to give Richard credit; he did have the balls to go in the hole for six grand before winning the eight grand. Balls??? Well, after all, he did have his life handed to him by his father, which isn't exactly fair, but who said life is fair anyway? The rich get richer. It makes my $280 gambling story sound a little not worth telling.

As Jack says, "A man has got to know his limitations." I'm pretty sure he stole that line from Clint Eastwood. Clint said it in the *Dirty Harry* movies, but Jack would say it as though it was his own.

Have you seen the movie *What About Bob?* It's a funny movie! Anyway, Carl's company paid for it along with the hotel room.

I went to the art district in Dallas the following day, but everything was closed except for the aquarium. The aquarium in Dallas was lame; it wasn't half as good as the one in Tennessee. The aquarium experience somewhat summed up downtown Dallas—disappointing mostly, except for the West End. One night, Carl and I went to Outback Steak House. The best part was the Outback Lager, which was really good, and the fact that they played Clapton made it taste even better.

    I had a good time with Carl. He has a great laugh and a dry British sense of humor that I find amusing. Carl was leaving the next day, so I needed to plan my next destination-X. My parents have some friends from back East, Will and Ann, who lived in Dallas-Fort Worth. Will and Ann would kill me if they found out I was in their neighborhood and didn't call or stop by.

    When I called their house, Ann convinced me to stay overnight but, when Will found out I was in town, he insisted that I stay at least a few days. I told them I didn't want to impose, and he said, "You're family and I don't want to hear another word about it." His words rang in my head and made me feel really special… I know he meant every word of it. I've known Will since I was a little kid. As a matter of fact, Will bought me my first baseball glove. There are events in life you never forget, and you never forget your first glove. It was a dark brown Wilson baseball glove. Will is a New Yorker, born and bred, and, as I remember, he always loved the family stuff. I also remember that he would come over to our house for Sunday dinner; he loved my mother's cooking and PASTA! Man, he could put away pasta with the best of the Italians—you would have thought they were going to stop making pasta the way he shoveled it down.

    They have one son, Billy, who was just a little boy when I last saw him but now he's in high school and taller than his old man. Billy was named after his old man obviously, and I was named after mine. I remembered as a kid, Will used to always use the expression, "your old man." He'd say, "Put your old man on the phone," or "Is your old man home?" or "You're just like your old man." I remember as a kid not liking that expression very much, but now, it's kind of growing on me. Everything changes.

Ann wanted me to teach her how to make fettuccine Alfredo. It was my pleasure, and I showed her a variation by adding shrimp and mushrooms.

My rules for cooking lessons are simple and as follows:
1. Wash your hands.
2. Get a drink—beer, wine, or your favorite cocktail will do.
3. Don't forget the instructing chef's drink— VERY IMPORTANT!
4. Let it all hang out!

The whole family raved about how good the food was—we all ate as if they were going to stop making pasta. We were all stuffed, and Will said we should open a restaurant together.

Family and friends—definitely a big part of what life is all about. Will and Ann treated me like a king who was returning home. They fed me, took me sightseeing, gave me a wonderful room to crash out in, and made me feel like family. They were genuinely happy for me to be there with them and just as genuinely sad to see me go. They wanted me to stay forever it seemed, but it was time...I thanked and hugged them good-bye after four days of their generosity.

Hopefully, someday I will be able to show them the same type of hospitality they showed me.

    I hope you like the latest picture.
    Smile, my brown-eyed Guy.
    You're in my thoughts... I love you.
    Nick
    -FeenX

February 1994
Guadalupe Mountains, Texas

The Capitan

—FeenX

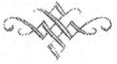

Road Recipe

Fettuccine Alfredo—Pay attention! Don't screw the pooch!
(A classic that reminds me of my father)

Ingredients:
- Fettuccine
- Butter
- Heavy cream
- Parmesan
- Salt and pepper
- Egg yolk

Directions:
1. Combine and reduce the butter, cream by 1/3rd.
2. Add Parmesan until smooth—low heat.
3. S&P to taste
4. Add Pasta and, when mixed thoroughly, take off the heat and mix in the egg yolk quickly (or you will have fettuccine and creamy cheesy scrambled eggs—doesn't sound so bad!) and serve.

Optional add-ins:
Shrimp
Mushrooms

Suggestions:
Cocktail: Skyy vodka on the rocks with a lime
Wine: Pinot Grigio, Pinot Noir
Beer: Long Trail Ale, Lone Star, Abita beer
Music: "The Good Life" by Tony Bennett

Chapter 8

Madman on the Highway

Written Journal Entry
February 26, 1994
Memories

    Cooking with Ann and talking with Will about opening a restaurant reminded me of my professional cooking roots. Another defining moment of my existence was when I quit my first real job after college. I was busting my ass off in a classy, Italian, Goodfellas joint, overlooking the Throgs Neck Bridge in Queens. The stories I could tell you about the people who worked and dined in that place are for another time. A quick little teat to suckle: after crazy-busy nights, to let off steam, the big shot chefs and the owner used to try to shoot the lights out on the bridge from the top of the restaurant with no regard for the cars or the people in them—Nice!

    I worked my way up through the ranks in a short time. I started as a Pantry Bitch making salads and cold appetizers, then I moved up to the pasta station, and I finally worked the sauté station on busy nights. Everything was paid in cash, and I started at $300 a week. On payday, the boss would walk by and pull out a roll of bills and peel off three and that would be that—no federal, no state, no social security, no disability, no nothing. He might as well have been counting out three dollars with the carefree way he paid me from his pile. The big shot chefs were making the real money—$800 to $1000 a week in cash. So, it took as much time and effort as it would take to count out ten dollars for them.

After a long summer and a short fall, I started feeling that I wasn't getting paid my fair share. One reason I was being pushed up so fast was because the kitchen staff turned over as fast as the dupes came in on busy nights, and they continued to pay me Pantry Bitch salary. Considering that I lived an hour away from the restaurant, tolls both ways on the bridge and gas were cutting into the money that Uncle Sam wasn't getting to wet his beak. I approached the boss and naively shook him down for an additional $100 a week. I felt pretty good about my performance; it was a big power play for me at the time.

After the busy holiday season was over (eighty-hour, six-day work weeks), the manager called me into the basement.

"The boss said he's taking your raise back."

"What?" I asked in disbelief. "How much is he taking back?"

"The whole raise, you're back to your original salary," he said, knowing that I'd walk out.

"That's nice. I guess the big boss doesn't have the balls to tell me that himself. Well, fuck him then! And, congratulations to you, I guess you can add a new title to your name besides Boss's Bitch—Pantry Bitch!"

I had pride, I had balls, I had attitude. I bought into the whole egotistical idea that I was a chef on the rise—someone to be respected. I wasn't going to let anyone treat me as though I were worthless.

I called my mother and grandmother in that order. I was looking to be commended for maintaining my dignity by having respect for myself. Instead, driven by their fear and shortsightedness, my grandmother assisted my mother in my gelding.

"Oh, Nick, I'm so disappointed in you. Are you crazy? How could you walk out of your job like that? What are you going to do for money? Can you get your job back if you apologize? This is a big mistake that will ruin your life." The Doomsday Machine cried, "The sky is falling, the end of the world is upon us."

All I heard was you are worthless, you chose poorly, you should take it in the ass when people are abusing you, the security of a job and money is worth more than your self-respect and dignity. I guess over time, pumping fear into your head can take hold. My mother can't even see this because her mother did a good job in the shrinking of her head. My grandmother came from a long line of headshrinkers, and I'm trying to end the cycle.

Audio Journal from the Car

February 27, 1994
Mood: Content—I'm not alone

Afternoon...
Testing, testing... Bye-bye, Will and Ann.
Well, it's 1:30 p.m. and I'm just leaving Will and Ann's house. It's been great!
I just saw my first cactus in Texas. The cactus isn't the standing fork cactus that I would like to photograph; it's the bush-like cactus.
Observation: it's not as flat as I've heard because I still see mountains, but I'm sure it will be.
In the background Rush Limbaugh is on the radio. This country has so much to offer... There's different scenery, different climates, different people, different cultures—if I had never left, I'd never know any of it even existed!
I just thought of a book idea that has to do with The Boys: me, Richard, Jack, and Paul. We all have different personalities, but we are all like washwomen with ovaries. We act like yentas, women, we all have different points of views, and we react to situations differently. I think it would make a good book or movie...
Some expressions from Texas: a guy is Bubba; hence, President Bubba. And a girl is Sissy. "Sissy, I apologize all the way back to the first time I hit you." As John Travolta said in *Urban Cowboy*.
One thing of note—the sun is mucho hot, it's cool outside but the sun is beating on my chest in the car—burning!
I need to get my father out of the stock market and into the real estate game...

I'm driving past this golf course right now, I don't see any grass, but people are playing. It looks like the whole course is sand—Odd, but it looks pretty cool.

There is a chick in front of me in a Mitsubishi 2000 and the license plate reads, 'EZ2LUV' Hoo-fucking-ha!

Yikes! Heart attack! Heart attack! Cop coming the other way just fucking… bam! All over my shit! Slammed on the brake and right by! Shit! Talk about wake-up call! Talk about heart attack!

Stink Creek Road: what a name. Like Bush Creek Road we passed a while back…

Talked to Paul today—he's back from Africa, or as he likes to say, he's back in-country. Such a nut.

Funny observation: I'm so far out west, the rest stop consists of three picnic tables and a shaded awning that goes over it. No building, no bathrooms, no… just unbelievable.

I'm thinking about The Boys and our friendship, maybe we're all still friends and everything because we've seen each other's penises. It's a possibility… I guess in life the older you get the less likely you are to see your friends' penises. Having seen someone's penis back when they were in high school creates a certain unmentionable bond. Maybe that's it.

The amazing part about this drive is I've been going for basically four hours now in a straight line and I haven't run into anything. It's just straight… nothing but straightness.

Just like I stopped in my first ghost town. It's pretty cosmic.

I think I see prairie lands now—tumble weed potential.

Right now I'm lost in Texas, East Bumfuck, and it really is Bumfuck. You get lost in one of these fucking towns and man there is nobody around and it's like fucking unbelievable. Holy shit!

The weirdest thing about the area I'm in is that I finally figured out where I'm going.

Ah, nice sunset…

Flatter than shit! The cool part is you don't have to look up to see the sky. The sky is right there touching the land—they meet, you see it, you can almost grab it with your hand. This illusion doesn't only happen in front of you, but everywhere in all directions. Your view is two feet of land and ten feet of sky.

My car is my earthship.

It's night and I just saw a million jackrabbits on the road—it's unbelievable!

KD Lang "Miss Chatelaine" is on the radio.

"Just a kiss just a kiss"

It's 8:16 p.m., and I have to tell you it's a bit scary. I don't know where the fuck I am. East Bumfuck Texas close to the Mexican border somewhere I'm guessing. I'm an hour away from Carlsbad, on backcountry roads. Following signs. Um… if I were to get stuck—Fuck, if anyone were to get stuck, there's nothing for millions of miles… Umm. I'm getting a bit anxious but supposedly I'm on the right road. This truly is the road less traveled that I'm fucking on right now, I'll tell you that!

March 1, 1994

9:20 a.m.
It's a beauty day eh! Called Allen to see where he is in conjunction to my travel plan and he said, "Come on down through New Mexico way!

Now that I see this place in the daylight, there's just nuthin'. Nuthin'! It looks like places that Clint Eastwood would have ridden through for Christ's sake! It's the desert.

I'm seeing a mountain range that doesn't even look real, it looks so unbelievable. It's almost like the land is so angry from the heat it's created all this prickliness, I don't know, there's cactus everywhere, the earth's skin is beyond burnt and calloused. The grass is harsh, the trees are bristly, and everything is rough!

Just turned 100,000 miles on the old earthship… Pearl Jam's "I'm Still Alive" is on the radio again!

Here are a couple of tips about tips. I just went into a photo store near Carlsbad Caverns, talked small to the old lady to see if she had any photo tips for the caverns. I asked her about the difference between Kodak Extra film versus plain Kodak film. She's like, "Oh, that's a great film!" Fuck her! Of course extra is better than the original version of the same film, I know the extra is good quality film. Asshole! What else, oh, she tells me something else convoluted that I don't even remember! Then she charged me twice as much as I would pay a mile down the road. Then she tells me I can take pictures without a flash in the caverns if I use fast speed film. Is she out of her fucking mind? She didn't give me one tip about taking pictures in the caverns and charged me way too much… You get what you pay for!

I'm Still Alive!

Back in Texas. There was this unbelievable haze in the morning. It's kind of weird. It's not haze, it's the wind blowing all this dust and dirt around and it looks like haze. That's why they say the rain is good for keeping all the "stuff" on the ground, not in the air.

The United States is one giant pussy just waiting to get fucked!

Live life on your own terms, or don't.

There ain't jack shit down in the southern part of New Mexico.

Last night, for dinner, I had to settle for Kentucky Fried Chicken, because that was the best place to actually sit down and eat dinner.

It's the grand premiere of the movie Cliffhanger—it's just opening here! It's showing at a one-movie house in the middle of nowhere.

I need to get on my mother. Texaco is pumping 86 octane as regular gas. Their super is only 90 octane. And the price is $1.24 when right down the street it's $1.12. What's up with that?

I'm so desperate I will listen to any dumb song on the radio that's not country. Listen to this dang song:

Stephen Bishop "On and On" is on the radio.

*"He just keeps on trying
And he smiles when he feels like crying"*

I must be losing my mind because right now, "On and On" sounds like a pretty good song...

✦ ✫ ✸

March 2, 1994

Morning:
It's another beautiful mornin', I'll tell you that! I just got finished listening to Melissa Etheridge, the one from her first album. "Everybody's got a reason to abandon their plan..."

Melissa Etheridge "Precious Pain" is on the radio.

> *"Empty and cold but it keeps me alive*
> *I gave it my soul so that I could survive*
> *Keeping me safe in these chains"*

Awesome song!

Late morning:
Now, I feel like Ansel Adams looking at El Capitan in the Guadalupe Mountains. I'm all by myself in the beautiful middle of, basically, the wilderness. It is the wilderness—this is really awesome.

The other side of the Guadalupe Mountains is even more beautiful than the side I was just on. Unbelievable! It's gorgeous. It's beautiful. If it's this beautiful here, I can't imagine what the Grand Canyon is like.

Early afternoon:
I can't believe everyone here looks like Mexicans. Hmm, that's odd!

Late afternoon:
Now, all I see for miles is sand. Sand everywhere and flat, flat, flat. No bushy bushes hanging out. This must be where they have the land speed records where the ground is so dry, so flat and thirsty it cracks—it's pretty cool!

Tip: Remember, when you're on a journey, don't just look in front of you but also look behind to see where you've been. It's just so

unbelievable! Every so often, I turn around and can't believe my eyes. It's so beautiful!
6:30 p.m.
Wait a minute. Now that I think about it, maybe that area was where they were testing atomic bombs, because we went right back to the bushy bushes… Like a whole section of life was snuffed out of the landscape.

I feel uneasy right now, like total destruction, like a wind could be coming in front of me and sweep me away… I would be gone without a trace with all the bushy bushes, animals, and elements.

You have to ask yourself how does life *exist* here? I just passed a cemetery. There was nothing but sand on top with dinky little flowers, no head stones on top, and every two feet another flower. Looks pretty pathetic.

March 3, 1994
Morning:
Now I've seen everything: a BYOB titty bar in the middle of fucking nowhere. But how can you beat that (why would you even try?), drink whatever you want…
12:45 p.m.
I just got out of the car in El Paso and it's HOT! First time on this trip I've been anywhere that's been hot. I'm sweating! Texas, El Paso cops drive Firebirds, including the Screaming Eagles painted on 'em. Another cool thing about the cop cars: their windows are smoked black and you can't see boo… Oh, by the way, I was just saved again by the radar detector; that's what spurred that little outburst.

Pink Floyd "Breathe" is on the radio.

"Breathe, breathe in the air"

I just drove through the entire city of El Paso. What a dump! Looking into the house to the left of me, I don't know what the hell they think they're doing. But it's a DUMP! Small, it's a small dump. Like the town I grew up in…

1:45 p.m.

Cops are swarming for whatever God-knows-what reason, in this area. That was the fifth cop.

It's so dusty out, I have the windows open and my fingernails are filled with dirt. It's disgusting dirty just from the air. Unbelievable!

"I'm on the way to White Sands, a place in New Mexico where major bomb and missile testing takes place. It looks like those video games where you're flying through the desert and there are mountains everywhere. Pretty cool. Damn it! I'm losing this good radio station I finally found from El Paso, Texas.

Oooh, Oooh, that cop's on the way to capturing his man. He just blew by me!

1:57 p.m.

It's so amazing—everyone I see is wearing those black, back-support belts from Sears. Everyone, driving, working, sitting, walking… Even the children!

It's unbelievable!

WOWIE! Spectacular! I just saw this beautiful, amazing sunset and got a glimpse of paper-white sand dunes. Hopefully I caught it all on film. White Sands was a beautiful place. I'm glad for the time of the year. It wasn't that hot. The time of the day was perfect. I wish I could have traveled into the desert but I'll be able to do that at another desert. It was free. It was closed...

I'm making a major move. I'm going all the way to Santa Fe—looking at the very least a four- to five-hour drive. I need to do this more often, I need to start staying in more hostels and less hotels. Need to stop spending money needlessly.

Not only are there pawnshops but there is also a hockshop—tons of misfortune to capitalize on here. Unbelievable!

This road I'm on tonight is one dark motherfucking road to nothing, I haven't passed one thing in miles. It's black as pitch, every once in a while someone comes the other way. Small narrow road, no dividing lines, very dark, very uncertain.

Oh, here it is, the song I sing to bust on my father.

Harry Chapin "Cat's in the Cradle" is on the radio.

> *"Little boy blue and the man on the moon*
> *When you comin' home son?*
> *I don't know when, but we'll get together then son*
> *You know we'll have a good time then"*

A sad song that I actually pray doesn't become reality for me and my dad...

11:30 p.m.

I finally made it into Santa Fe. It took me five long hours...

Written Journal Entry

1:00 a.m.

Wiped Out

My plan when I got into Santa Fe was to stay in a motel for a few dollars more—that was what I wanted to do but didn't. Instead I went to the Santa Fe hostel and it was, to say the least, interesting.

The hostel manager was Jamaican and he showed me around. I noticed a posting board for messages—a place where people were exchanging help for need and vice versa. Really cool that people will help each other out when in need. Finally he got around to showing me the available room, which I could potentially share with four other people. Two people were already sawing away.

Before bedding down, I decided to go out and get something to eat. Figuring I'd stake my claim and unpack when I returned. I ended up eating some horrendous Denny's grand-slam-crap breakfast at 12:30 a.m. for God knows what reason.

When Nick-er-ella returned from the ball, somebody was sleeping in his bed!

Shit! Somebody was in the bottom bunk. I should have never left without marking my territory. I should never assume that someone wouldn't check in after me. I should have set up my bed! I should not have eaten that godforsaken, gonna-give-me-ptomaine-poisoning breakfast after midnight. So then I had to climb to the top bunk, which was sagging a foot and a half in the middle, shaped like Mrs. Bates died in it—I figured it would be great fun for my back.

Anytime I move even a little bit the whole bed shook including the guy underneath—hahaha, it was kind of funny!

Oh, before I forget, I saw a movie about *502 Los Alamos*, it was very interesting—it's where the first atomic bomb was made.

With all the coughing and hacking that was going on in my hostel room, I figured I was going to catch the plague for sure!

The Irie guy said that at the hostel we all had to pitch in with chores in the morning. I thought I was going to end up scrubbing fucking toilets!

How was I supposed to sleep?

I was anxious about being a *family* with strangers and the chores thing—I was such a freak! I had nothing better to worry about.

Audio Journal from the Car

March 4, 1994

    Waking up in Sante Fe! …Crisp clean air, you can see your breath!
    Man! Unbelievable! There is snow on the damn mountains! I didn't see any of these splendors last night. Fucking unbelievable! How gorgeous! Goddam! Beautiful day! Stayed in a hostel last night! Pretty hostile! Hahaha. It's just so beautiful! I'm sorry I am unable to come up with better words to describe this. It's time to thank God… Thank you for this natural visual stimulation, thank you for this feeling of exhilaration thank you for this opportunity to experience it. I never would have had this opportunity if not for… Wow, I'm feeling a wave of sadness! I don't know. I would give it all up for… Fuck, I miss Laura a lot!
    Come on! Refocus!
    So this morning I get up, go to the bathroom, plan on taking my time, only one other person left and he was sleeping. I stink, haven't taken a shower in two days. I jumped into the shower and realized I didn't have a towel, what the fuck do I do? Adapt! Overcome! So I dried myself with my shirt. Roughing it and loving it! I was dripping everywhere. I policed up my frags and sleeping bag. Time to face the music—go get my chores. I walk in, everybody's already up eating breakfast at these primitive *Planet of the Apes* tables, the fireplace was roaring. Everybody was hippy dippy and from different countries, very cool! I'm a nervous wreck because everyone was looking at me—relax, relax, nobody's really looking.

I go to the chore list and it's like wake up early get whatever you want, wake up late and get bathrooms and toilet bowls! Oh boy! My hope was to get one that would be the least disgusting. I have to say it really wasn't that bad, the worst part was the mere thought of me scrubbing other people's piss and shit in and around the toilet bowls. Yuck!

I finally started warming up to my new surroundings and new comrades. After toilet-cleaning detail was over, I met Shelly, a nice girl, who was in charge of the hostel during the day. Shelly was a beautiful girl, maybe 19 or 20 years old, with blonde hair, very blessed in the chest area. Nice! She smelled like clean fresh air in the mountains above the forest. Nice! I would guess, by the clothes she wore, that she was into the grunge scene, which could suggest hairy underarms. Nice?

In the common room they were all trying to kill this bug. I tried not to draw attention from the fearful looking exterminators and said to myself, "Self, don't make eye contact, I don't want to kill the bug."

I really enjoyed this hostel. I might even go back to spend another night instead of staying at a motel. After all, the Sante Fe International Hostel has a little piano room with games. Everything is old, decrepit, and dilapidated. Charming, is what it was! And so was Shelly!

The mountains are spectacular! I see plateaus, I see mountains, it's just all very unbelievable, and this is so awesome. I'm on my way to Bandelier National Monument to see cliff dwellings and shit.

The people from the adjoining room were banging around at like 5:30 a.m. all backpacked and ready to go hiking in the mountains. All they carry with them is the stuff on their back and they just go from place to place. It's wild, and really what I should be doing. But I just don't know.

My roommates' names were Hans and Lu Chin. We shared the room to sleep in, a bathroom, which was also located inside our room, and now conversation over breakfast.

Lu Chin was from Japan and he said, "Ohayo," which means, good morning in Japanese. Hans sprechen zie, "Guten Morgen," which means good morning. Hans had to reeducate me, I had forgotten most of what I learned studying German for two years in junior high, "Guten Tag" means hello all day long. And then there is Nick Anthony: "How you doin'?" So we have: Ohayo, Guten Morgen, and How you doin'? Unbelievable! The United Nations right here in Sante Fe speaking the international language of good morning!

For breakfast, there were all kinds of cereal; you did have to buy your own milk, but a lot of stuff here is free. Sweet!

Right now:

They have a local brewery! Rio Bravo.

I'm climbing mountains for Christ's sake, it's unbelievable! It's gorgeous and I'm taking pictures with my camera and mind. Everyone's doing their own thing: mountain biking, hiking, and climbing the face of mountains with ropes. Oh man, I'm standing on the edge, there's no guardrail. If you fall off, you're done. The Rio Grande, man oh man, White Rock. I don't know why they call it White Rock, it's black! Maybe that's why! Gorgeous! I've been driving up and down Route 502—eerie.

Cranberries "Linger" is on the radio.

"And I'm in so deep
You know I'm such a fool for you
You got me wrapped around your finger"

Good song but the words are kind of stupid, don't you think? Wrapped around your finger, do you have to let it linger, do you have to let it linger…

2:27 p.m.

It's cool to be polite. Saying hello when you see somebody, smile when you look at somebody—and they are not like, "What are you looking at? What do you want from me?" You know, N.Y. normal, with attitude. It's like, "Hello, we are humans sharing the planet, shouldn't we be nice?" Not "Hello, give me sex or money or your wallet!"

Line from the *Crying Game*: "Why did you eat me? Mr. Fox said to Mr. Alligator."

"It's in my nature." I'm sorry; it's in my nature. Being gay, is genetic not a choice, not something to be helped, it's just the way it is—get over it!

James Taylor's "You've Got a Friend" is on the radio.

"Winter, spring, summer, or fall,
All you have to do is call
And I'll be there, yeah, yeah, yeah"

Thank God, for this spectacular weather, this is a perfect time of the year to be traveling around this beautiful culturally diverse, multi-climatic country.

Ah Bandelier—Indian ruins. Uhhh, I'm just not into it. I don't like Indian ruins! What can I say? I just don't care for them.

Madman on the Highway—Letter 5
March 5, 1994

Hi, Laura,

Sorry I haven't written in a while; I've been driving like a madman!

As I drove away from Will and Ann's slice of suburban life and safety, I realized that I was headed toward the largest step of my journey. I was pretty much flying by the seat of my pants from that point onward. I had the maps, but they were just that—maps. I was relying on a two-dimensional flat piece of paper, a country mapped out by someone I didn't even know, to be my guide.

I left Dallas-Fort Worth about 1:30 p.m. and was faced with eight hours of the most boring-ass driving that you can't even begin to imagine, straight through the butt-hole that is Northwest Texas. There is literally nothing for miles except this rough beat-up land. This land has nothing else to do but sit and wait for whatever wicked torrid elements nature is going beat on it with. Rest easy, though, you don't have to worry about this land; you could tell it can deal with anything. This land had been through rough times before the scars were apparent. There isn't anything nature can dish out that this land can't handle. Obviously, you can tell the drive was very long and boring from my silly stories.

There was one stretch where the sun was blasting through the windshield so fiercely that it felt as if the glare were burning holes in my eyeballs. I had to pull over. I couldn't see a thing, except for spots, even with my sunglasses on.

I think the only part of the trek through Butt-hole-O'Texas worth mentioning was stopping at any given gas and sip. Your car can belly up to the car bar, order a drink while you are inside the station buying beer or whiskey and a handgun with as many bullets as you can carry. Put all the charges on the Texaco card and be on your way before your car is even finished whetting its whistle. No waiting—how scary is that?

The first night while driving through the empty Texas highway there was this evil moon. The moon was so bright that it created sharp silhouettes of mountains and clouds, nearly taking up the entire skyline; it was eerie but very, very cool.

Occasionally, I get freaked out late at night on these long endless roads—black-paved paths that all looked the same after a while. There were many times I didn't see another car or any sign of life for hours. I was completely alone with my glorious imagination riding shotgun. I wondered what I would do if I broke down one of those nights. Would I get out of my car and try to find help or would I just sleep in the car and worry about it in the safety of daylight? Luckily, I haven't had to do anything but wonder about what I would do. So far, so good. Knock-on-wood: knock, knock.

The skies were so amazing at night because the land out here is very flat. It's pitch black, and these twinkling stars are everywhere all the way down to the horizon, flickering away, it's very cool!

After endless hours of driving, I finally got to my destination, a hostel in Carlsbad, New Mexico. A youth hostel in Carlsbad was a thirty-

Madman on the Highway

minute drive outside the city limits. I was exhausted, but somehow I managed to get there in one piece. The hostel was more expensive than the guidebook said, and on top of everything, it was a scary dump. No one seemed to be around. This hostel looked like the kind of place that you could take a person and butcher them up, in good-ole Charlie fashion. You could chop them up in little pieces for the rats to eat. Nobody would hear, smell, or care about anything. As tired as I was, I demanded my money back, got back on my horse in one piece, and drove back to the city limits. For $5 more I stayed in a motel with a bed that had sheets, cable TV, a hot shower, and most importantly, peace of mind.

Although it was a cool experience, I blew my knees out while hiking down Carlsbad Caverns. Before I climbed down the bat cave, a park ranger asked me whether I had heart problems or any physical disabilities or knee problems. I said "No, no, and no!" Who the fuck has knee problems? Well, by the time I got to the bottom of this unbelievable cave, my knees were on fire. I didn't think I would make it, but I was glad I struggled through it. The stalagmites and stalactites looked like something out of a freaky science fiction movie; I couldn't believe that it was all natural. The caverns in Carlsbad were spectacular! It's hard to imagine that this vast space could exist 750 feet underground. Mother Nature created this spectacular spectacle without any help from man or beast. It made me realize that a lot of science fiction is based on natural things.

Side note: When I got to the bottom of the cave, I pulled out my camera and tested my flash. Guess what happened? Nothing. NOTHING! It didn't work! Batteries, right? WRONG!

I lugged this damn flash and extra batteries all over this country just in case someday, somewhere, I might need it, and the one time I do need it, it doesn't work!
WOW! That felt good, thanks for letting me vent. Anyway, I did all that I could do without the flash—time will tell or, should I say, the pictures would tell.
Unfortunately, I did miss the one event at the cave that would have truly been a photo opportunity of a lifetime. I missed the flight of a billion bats flying in or out of the cave hole for feeding, because it was the wrong time of year—it would have been an incredible sight!
The next couple of days were very busy. I drove back down into Texas to see the Guadalupe Mountains and El Capitan. Unbelievable! I hope my pictures come out the way I envisioned them in my head.
You should have seen me on the side of the road with my camera, jacket blowing in the breeze, camel-hair brush sticking out of my pocket, contrast filters blazing in and out, and cable release firing. Totally Ansel Adams—type material.
I left Texas midday again, this time to go to White Sands, New Mexico. My goal was to get there before sunset, which I just managed to do. The sand there is really white; I'll send you some in a film container. I was glad to be able to witness the burnt-orange sun melting into the white sand like a giant Creamsicle. I got there just in time. It was beautiful. I was hiking and climbing, all kinds of good stuff, feeling like the true outdoorsman.
After the sun went "night night," I had to make decisions that I've been getting used to making on a moment's notice since I had no set

schedules. Where to next? How far am I willing to drive? How far am I capable of driving at this time? Decision time.
 Destination: Albuquerque, New Mexico, it is!
 Albuquerque is actually a rather small town with a very big name. Everyone at the southern end looked Mexican, and everyone at the northern end looked Indian. I have driven through and past many Indian reservations throughout New Mexico; I had no idea there were so many. I was kind of excited to see Albuquerque after hearing that unusual name for so many years. Bugs Bunny made making "a left at Albuquerque" famous. He was trying to get to Pismo Beach for clams.
 I was looking for a place to crash for the night so I could explore in the morning. As a child, and now as an adult, I have no idea what Bugs was talking about. After all the talk, I just ended up driving through little old Albuquerque to get to Santa Fe.
 Anywho, it was very late at night when I arrived at the Santa Fe hostel, or commune in this particular case. Of course, the hostel membership that I had wasn't good for this hostel either. I had to pay the full price of $27—again! Bob Marley was the hostel manager with dreads, groovy clothes, and the "Ya-mon," Irie attitude. There was a living room with board games and books, dining area, storeroom, clean-up-after-yourself kitchen, laundry room supplied with detergent (pretty good perk), and finally the old bunkhouse that even had a bathroom in it. It was a far cry from the hellhole at Carlsbad! But...
 The bed was literally only 2 feet wide. I almost pulled this rickety bunk bed apart trying to climb up into it because there was

no ladder, but I finally got to my perch. I put my shoes under my head as a pillow, but I didn't take any other clothing off, not even my glasses. I just laid there like a frozen mummy because I was afraid of falling off. It was warm so I slept on top of my sleeping bag, besides it would have been too noisy to squirm into it. I feared for my physical and mental health until morning. All the noise, noise, noise! People were creaking, coughing, sneezing, talking, and milling around like the living dead, all night long. I thought for sure I would get sick, have a broken back, and have my brains eaten all by morning.

Every hostel is run differently. At this one, the people staying and paying at the hostel were required to do chores in the morning. We all had to do our part like we were a big family. I did like the concept of everyone helping out.

In the morning, I met Burgomeister from Germany, "Guten Morgen. Wie Gehts" and Lee Chong from Japan, "Ohayo." We each spoke different languages and were able to communicate with each other—it was great!

The girl in charge of the hostel during the day told me about a bunch of places to see while I was in the Santa Fe area: White Rock Mountain, which was probably the inspiration for the White Rock soda brand, because it looked just like it. There was a spectacular view of the mountains and the Rio Grande River from the top—it was magnificent! Bandelier National Monument, on the other hand, was about cliff dwellings—remnants of an ancient civilization long, long ago—just so-so in my opinion.

So it was time to get out of Dodge, with that decree, it was once again time to make the call about Destination X. I could have stayed in Santa Fe for the night, but it was a bit of a dump. The high point of Santa Fe might have been the hostel; at least there were colorful people around; it had its own culture and it was organized.

Don't get me wrong, Santa Fe is beautiful because the mountains are covered in snow, the orange-colored adobes are everywhere, the skies are deep blue, and the air is cold and crisp. But, other than that, it sucks. I don't know why people would say, "It's an up-and-coming place to live." There was nothing to do, but chill out.

I'm leaving for Durango, Colorado because it's only eight hours away and near Mesa Verde National Park, then I can easily loop down into Arizona.

Okay then, that sounds like a game plan to me!

> Winter, spring, summer or fall,
> I'll be there...
> Love you,
> Nick
> -FeenX

March 1994
Carlsbad Caverns, N.M.

Yikes! It's Scary Down Here!
—FeenX

Chapter 9

Mile High

Written Journal Entry

March 6, 1994

Bunker Mentality

Observations, ramblings, and the state of mind of a madman spending too much time driving and talking to himself in the car...

While traveling through some of the lonelier and less-fortunate places, I thought about periods of famine and sacrifice. When I left home, there was a definite concern about running out of money while on my journey—how much money would I be able spend on food, lodging, gas, and film before I was out of cash, and before I would have to go to work? I think about being homeless, wondering where my next meal would come from, where I will rest my head and wash my feet, because I don't know how long I will be away. These thoughts gave me a Bunker Mentality. A Bunker Mentality is when you have to settle down in a bunker and do what you have to until the war is over—no splurging, no extras, no fancy feasts. Being clever, crafty, and borderline criminal—relying on your instincts could be the difference between getting by and suffering.

Somewhere along the way I managed to hit a pothole. At first I didn't notice that hitting the pothole loosened the exhaust—due to the noisy rain that pounded the roof of the car. When the rain stopped the car sounded more like a tank and wasn't drivable because of all the noise it made. I didn't need to be hassled by the police. The muffler place wanted a ridiculous amount of money to fix it. The money would cut into my funds for eating and sleeping, so I came up with a creative solution. I went to Sears the *store with more—to return*, as I liked to say—and bought a floor jack, two ramps to enable me to get under the car, and tools to assist me. I spared no expense because I knew that I wouldn't be keeping any of these items. After I fixed my car to be like new, I returned everything to Sears—no questions asked, no hassles, and no cutting into my eating and sleeping money. I even changed the oil as long as I was there and saved myself that money. Everything was returned in the sparkling shape in which it was purchased. Overcoming and conquering obstacles is a prerequisite in the hospitality industry and a technique that saved my ass often. In Bunker Mentality World, a flawed system is a system to be taken advantage of, especially if no one is getting hurt. I reserved this technique for absolute emergencies. I will admit that I used it one time because I wanted to see whether I could get away with it and another time because it was easy and there was nothing they could do to stop me—it was their system after all, and nobody did ever get hurt.

I made a list, checked it twice, and looked for glutton and abuse. The young, pimply clerks rang up each item up with joy, calculating in their tiny heads how much commission they would be making on the sale. They would follow me around the store to carry whatever I touched. I could barely contain my laughter, knowing that I would never be paying for the items I was borrowing.

I would arrogantly return to the scene after a week or so of use, sometimes to the same clerk who sold me the merchandise in the first place. Out of boredom and hoping to get caught so that my genius could be recognized—but there was no crime being committed—everything was paid for then returned in the exact same shape it was borrowed in. It was super genius.

As meticulously as I unpacked my pirate's booty, I would repack it for return. I was careful to save every last piece of wrapping. Each wire was rebound; each widget was put back into its original bag and placed in its original spot in the box. Every piece of tape reattached; batteries replaced; and all manuals were folded, stuffed, and repacked with the original care that some person from Taiwan or China used to pack it with originally.

I considered myself a professional executing perfection. No one would be the wiser. No one would suffer the aggravation of missing pieces as I did on occasion because of some careless employee's incompetence or, worse, some inconsiderate hack attempting to do what I had turned into an art form.

"Hi, I would like to return these items," I said and smiled.

"Of course sir," said an eager Mr. Pimples. "Do you have the original receipt, sir?"

"Of course," I told Mr. Pimples, trying to make it as easy as possible.

"Is there anything wrong with it?"

"No."

"Has it been opened?"

"No."

"The reason you are returning it ...is?"

"Do I need a reason?" I asked, annoyed that my time was now being wasted.

"No, no sir you don't," he said, hoping that I wasn't going to report him to the manager.

"Okay then, no reason," I said.

"Here is your new receipt with the credit given to your card. Thank you for your patience. Thank you for shopping with us. Come again."

Mr. Pimples begged me to come back, as per management mandate.

"Thank you," I said. "I will."

Bunker Mentality has helped me through some lean and unknown times, but I think the reality of it was that I was just romanticizing the notion of being squalid. Truth be told, although I was alone on this trip, I was never really alone in the world. I knew I wouldn't go hungry, and I knew I could always find a place to rest my head and wash my feet. Credit cards go a long way!

Mile High—Letter 6
March 7, 1994

Hey, Laura,

When I got to Durango, Colorado, it looked like a winter wonderland—snow covered all the right places. Durango, I have to say, is a very, very cool town. My definition of cool town is: artsy, crafty, lots of high-atmosphere bars, gourmet eateries, shops, galleries, and maybe even a brewpub. Durango has them all plus the freshest air, the most amazing mountainsides with snow covered pine trees, and skiing!

By the time I settled in and got my bearings, all the places recommended by my travel guide were closed for the night. The only place in town open was called Fourquarts, where I ended up talking to Casey, this hippy-chick waitress from California.

Casey told me that she liked the small-town flair that Durango offered, as opposed to her California, and she also liked the Durango beer and skiing. Casey had long dirty blonde hair that hung all the way down to her ass. Her hair was so fine that if a breeze blew her hair in your face, the thin strands could get caught in your beard like a web. She reminded me of the girl, I think her name was Julie, from the "Mod Squad." I drank some Durango beer that was really very good!

Casey recommends that I go to the Carver's Bakery Café Brewery for freshly brewed beer and just-out-of-the-oven muffins and scones before I leave Durango.

Snow is just starting to fall, and I'm going to bed. Before I leave this wonderful town in the next couple of days, I must stop at the recommended brewery.

Mile High

Since I'm still getting over the Horror Hostel in Carlsbad and I'm still feeling a bit anxious from the "living dead" in Santa Fe, I'm staying in a hotel with a big bed and hot water for $28 dollars.

It is always comforting for me to be able to wash my hands after a long trip. My rationale is that if I look down and see that my hands are clean, then I am clean. I wonder if that's what Pontius Pilate was thinking at the time.

Haven't heard from you, tried calling numerous times.

I think about you everyday.

Love you,

Nick

—Feenx

March 1994
Four Corners Country

Sand and Totem
—FeenX

Chapter 10

Bakery and Brewery

Written Journal Entry

March 7, 1994

My Neurosis

    I don't know if it was the fresh snow laying on the ground in Durango or the wet black pavement shining through that reminded me of the day I picked up my new car from the dealer so many years ago. It could be that I was missing home or not missing some of the ridiculousness that goes on there. I love my mother, but some of her thought processes that affect me to this day are priceless.

    A perfect example of my mother's line of thinking:

    On my twenty-fifth birthday, I bought my first new car. I'm not talking about my first used car, and I'm not talking about getting a great deal from a relative. I'm talking about buying my first brand new car from a showroom dealer. I did all the research—read consumer reports, did actual test drives, comparison-shopped, talked with people who owned the same car, and so on. I bought a candy-apple red Nissan 240SX, with both the sport and luxury packages. When I sat in the driver seat, I felt like I was in the space shuttle, and two people could sit in the back if they had to. What did I care about sitting in the back? It was my car; I would be the driver, who cared about the comfort of the back seat? It was dream come true. I was going to buy it—on my own—I was a man making my own decisions. So, on my twenty-fifth birthday, I called the five dealers I had been talking to and made my pitch.

Taking the lowest price quoted, I said, "It's my birthday and I'm going to sign a contract with the dealership today that gives me the best price. The lowest price I have so far is $18k. If you can give me a better deal, I will be down there to sign on the dotted line in five minutes." I even negotiated like a professional.

I was so excited! I couldn't wait to show my parents the new car. I was so excited to see how excited they would be for me. I just knew they would be so proud and impressed. The day I picked up the car was cold and sunny with four inches of fresh snow melting on the wet black pavement, making it very bright out. The car glistened like a newly buffed ruby.

With a wide pained smile, my mother said, "There's not much room in the back for passengers."

Not really understanding her point, I said, with a touch of bravado, "What difference does it make how much room is in the back seat? I will be driving in the front seat!"

Continuing to suck even more air out of my sails, she said, "With only two doors, it will be difficult for people to get in and out, not to mention how you will struggle if you have groceries."

Being made to feel like I just made the biggest mistake of my life, I asked, "So, you don't like it?"

"No, no ... I like it, but I'm just saying, if you had to, how would you move a couch? Someday if you had to, how would you do it?"

How would I move a couch if I *had* to?—*someday?* I asked myself. *How could I move a fucking couch?*

I brought home my first, brand-spanking-new, super-sporty, shiny-red, leathered interior, too-small-in-the-back-to-be comfortable, can't-move-a-fucking-couch-if-I-*had*-to car, and my mother pissed all over the front seat.

Bakery and Brewery—Letter 7
March 8, 1994
Quick note from the brewery

Hey, Laura,

I know I just wrote you, but I had to write a quick note. I'm leaving Durango, Colorado but, I need to mention that it's even more beautiful in the daylight; talk about blue skies!

Snow is just starting to come down again on the mountains and the big green pine trees; it's spectacular—an extremely coooool town that you would love! Besides, the tchotchke shops and cafes, there are these granola-munching people who mill around all day as if they have nothing better to do than appreciate life, appreciate the natural splendor, appreciate the beer, and love Durango, Colorado!

I am writing to you as I sit in the Carver's Bakery Café Brewery. It's only 10 a.m., but I feel the need, or should I say, I feel that it is my responsibility to try their beer before I leave. This place was closed every time I tried to visit so this will be my last opportunity. While sipping a smooth Carver Colorado Trail Nut Brown Ale, I'm munching on a hot-out-of-the-oven banana nut muffin. What a fan-fucking-tabulous combination! I should be writing commercials. WOW! The beer must be going to my head.

Imagine the combination: bakery and brewery—maybe the beer went to their head. If you so desire, you can bring their beer home in jugs, and they will even refill it if you bring the jug back.

I want to try every selection they offer, but I don't think it would be prudent, because I have many hours of driving in front of me. Unfortunately, I have to say good-bye…

    Ciao,
    Nick

March 1994
Four Corners Country

Clap Hands! Clap Hands!
—FeenX

Chapter 11

Green Table

Audio Journal from the Car

March 8, 1994
Mood: Pumped!

10:45 a.m.
Testing, testing… Durango is one cool-ass town. Got in last night and didn't see much, but today the views are spectacular. Skies are blue, with fluffy white clouds showing through. We must be so high up. One place I wanted to go but was closed when I got in was the Carver's Bakery Café Brewery. Read about it in the travel guide. Ended up going to Farquarters, had burritos like in the book, just eh, but they did have Durango beer, which was very good! Slept in a nice bed.

Talked to Laura this morning and uh, thank God it was a good conversation. We haven't had a good conversation since before Myrtle Beach; seems like, about a month, month and a half ago. Yes it was. But, ah, talked about how it's going with her. Sometimes she feels good, sometimes she doesn't. She has recently been really sick. Laura told me to tell my mother she got the messages and hello and thanks but she just doesn't want to talk to anyone right now. Just like my mother said. Bottom line:

We had a good conversation. I got to tell her what I've been doing. She got to tell me what's been going on with her. God, I miss her, I miss her a lot. Um, I miss the day-to-day routines, as well. But at least I talked to her and it went well. I told her that I missed her a lot. Laura was like, "It was good talking with you and keep in touch," but she didn't, couldn't oh no, just wouldn't say it back! The only other thing I wanted to say but hadn't in a while was that I loved her. So I said it but she didn't reciprocate that either, but I don't care about that fact right now. I wanted to say it! It's what I wanted to do! I know she's not feeling well; she's out of it, I think.

I need to thank Mina for her advice and insight. Laura didn't even remember talking to me from the hospital. These are things I don't even think of or could understand. Laura said "happy birthday"; she's sorry she didn't get in contact with me. I'm just glad she remembered to say it. These little things mean a lot to me. Oh, wow, look at that hawk! It just flew out of nowhere and is so beautiful.

Anyway I did get to stop by the Carver's Bakery Café Brewery and Casey and my guidebooks were right—Right on! It was all really very good! I wasn't sure if they would serve me beer because it was just before 11 a.m., but they did—Sweet! They had a barley wine that I would have liked to try. I wish I could have tried all of them, but I did have to be on my way and I was driving.

Possible idea: Nick Anthony travels the country in so many days tasting so many beers. Might be a good idea for a book. There are a lot of good ideas—I just have to do them!

Anyway, Durango: cool town. I would like to revisit it. Someday, whenever that is…

There were some cool birds up here like blue jays…

As cool as everything I'm seeing is, oh man…I'm getting a hankering for wanting to go home. Right now, I'm beat, traveling from place to place. Not knowing where I'm going to go. Staying at hotels, staying at hostels, in tents, in my car. I miss my family. I miss my friends… I miss Laura.

Ah… I have to forge ahead—enough of that talk! Perfect song! Remember this song?

Joe Cocker "When the Night Comes" is on the radio.

"Hold on
I'll be back for you
It won't be long
But for now there's something else
That's calling me
So take me down a lonesome road"

Written Journal Entry
March 9, 1994
Boys Out in Town

 I've been thinking about the days before I left New York, it seems like forever ago. The night I had a farewell cocktail with The Boys was a classic, as so many nights with them were.

 They picked me up at 8:30 p.m. Jack drove, Richard rode shotgun, and Paul and I were in the back tending the cooler. Jack drove because due to the nature of his job he has a get-out-of-jail-free card. He tried one night to convince us how it was professional courtesy to allow fellow union members to drive under the influence, while it was fair to throw a commoner in the clink, forever changing their life. They handed me a libation and before I could put my seatbelt on, the four of us were partaking in a joyful tradition as old as our driver's licenses. As politically incorrect as this sounds, drinking while in the car was a pastime that we loved and held dear to our hearts. I loved it. I've always loved it.

 There is something about being on the road to nowhere, reaching into a full cooler, sifting through the ice, and cracking open a cold beer—the fresh breeze blowing through the car windows mixing with the smell of newly opened beer, good friends singing along with the radio when they're not ragging on each other, and roaming the miles of wide open road. It made no difference whether it was an old country road or a six-lane superhighway—as long as we didn't run out of road or beer, it was good. "Here's to good friends, tonight is kind of special..." It sounds like a commercial to me.

 I do understand why this sort of cabal is frowned upon by society. I certainly do not recommend this kind of behavior to anyone. Everyone has to be his own man and take responsibility for his actions. I have to include that in all the years of this sort of activity that we have been unbelievably lucky. We have avoided fatal accidents and serious altercations with the law. Drinking with my buddies in a car reminds me of my childhood, of good times with good friends—something I hope I'll never forget.

Just for clarification: I'm not talking about getting drunk and getting behind the wheel, I'm talking about drinking and driving—there is a subtle difference between the two.

We live in a different time than when we were growing up. It wasn't as socially unacceptable as it is now. Something else to keep in mind, *sheep*: it started out, as "Friends don't let friends drive drunk." It's now "Friends don't let friends drink and drive." Do you see the difference?

My last night with The Boys was at Elmer Suds, a cool New York style pub with the ultimate selection of beer from around the world. We bellied up to the bar and had one selection after another. The cute bartender gave us passports so we could keep track of our trip around the globe.

We spent some time in the past, always guaranteed to bring tears of laughter down our faces. And we spent some time speculating about the future. We dragged the cute bartender into our little conversations like a squirrel with nuts. We pretty much dominated the bar; the few other patrons were noticeably annoyed that we took the attention of the person supplying their needs.

"I can't believe you're really leaving." Paul shook his head in disbelief.

"I'm proud of you," said Jack. "You're going out there and living life on your own terms. Most people are full of shit. What kind of honor is there in changing dollars?"

"This country was built on changin' dollars..." Paul quoted Tony Montana from *Scarface*, with his best Cuban accent. We were always quoting movies—it's too bad you can't get paid for quoting movies—we would be living large—what a honor.

"Ah, you're a fucking pussy for leaving us," Richard said. And then doing his best Nick impersonation, said, "Oh, Laura dumped my sorry-cheese-dick ass. Poor me, I'm going to run away, boo, hoo-hoo."

It's a tough group but don't wince or let any blood get in the water or you'll be in for a real shark attack.

"Good luck with your marriage, I hope you'll be as happy as I was," I said.

"Nice talk. Whose got the cards?" Paul asked hoping to get back some of his lost green.

"I can't afford to lose anything at this point," I said.

Richard, the luckiest bastard on the planet, said with a huge grin, "Sure you do—you still have your health, don't you? Get it out there."

"A man's got to know his limitations," Jack said.

"That's nice and original, Jack, now get your money out." Paul said trying to make up for a year's worth of losing all in a single bet.

"It's only money, for Christ sake," Richard said, knowing he would be going home with all our money—again.

"Fuck you!" the three of us told Richard in unison.

Richard and Paul have been cutting cards for money since high school. Back then, Jack and I would watch in disbelief as they would each pull out a hundred dollar bill and put it on the table. Each one would cut the cards and whoever had the high card would win. Richard would pick up the $200 and put it in his pocket and taunt Paul to go again. There were times when Paul would lose $300 to $500 in a matter of five minutes.

Richard and Paul always had cash rolling out of their pockets—crazy money as far as Jack and I were concerned. We all came from different cities around the county joined together by the Catholic high school our parents sent us to. Even though we shared the same school and religion, we came from different backgrounds—ethnic as well as financial. Jack and I came from the other side of the tracks and didn't have the same kind of resources as our rich friends. We were as big a part of the popular group as any one of them, though. Our friends didn't notice we were different that way—maybe that was because we were all necessary to make up the group for it to work. We did make fun of the differences we could see, though.

Audio Journal from the Car

March 10, 1994
Mood: Amazed

9:45 a.m.
Testing, testing, approaching heaven, weather is cold, sunny and crisp blue skies...

Spectacular views from this mountainous road in Mesa Verde. I feel like I have this whole peak to myself. God must be close. I've only passed one, maybe two other cars in the last 75 miles—that's it.

Sorry to interrupt, but it's worth mentioning again since it happens so infrequently—Laura kept saying she was glad I got her on the phone. And to keep in touch—I'm glad...

Gorgeous scenery, gorgeous day, speckles of snow! I have a new respect for the survival of humans.

"If life were simple, what would we do?" a substitute instructor once asked my class back in college. How true... If life were easy and nothing was a problem, what would we do— sit around and enjoy life all day! Hahahaha— somebody would have to do the difficult work—so life couldn't be simple for all.

No, it would get boring. I guess that's the point. There would be no high highs because there couldn't be any low lows, and how would you know the difference if you didn't have both ends of the spectrum?

I believe the exact expression was, "If life were perfect." Not just simple, but perfect.

I just can't stand that new Meatloaf song! I can't stand Meatloaf!

Today's a day I feel really good. Just good about myself, I guess. Woke up very positive.

I feel like I have the world by the balls, and it's up to me to make things happen.

One of my all-time favorite Eric Clapton songs, if not favorite by any artist. Yes, you look wonderful tonight!

Eric Clapton "Wonderful Tonight."

> *"I feel wonderful because I see*
> *The love light in your eyes.*
> *And the wonder of it all*
> *Is that you just don't realize how much I love you"*

EC's "Wonderful Tonight" is still on the radio, still riding high from the Laura convo—she said she was glad to hear my voice! She was excited, not angry, but happy! You could hear the smile in her eyes by her voice—you know what I mean...a very good day!

In 1994, I went on a sabbatical in search of life.

A lot of beautiful areas around here. I'm in Cortez, near Telluride. Telluride, from what I hear, is amazing, as in hoppin'! Well, that's what Casey, Casey from California says anyway.

One thing's for shit sure, the views are SPECTACULAR and inspirational. I am energized by the feeling of awe.

The Indians seem to have it made man. I'm talking about official Indians from America. There are Indians selling their wares up and down the highway. Shop after shop after shop! Jewelry shops, rugs shops, bead shops, silver shops, turquoise shops, tobacco shops. I'm not driving through a reservation so I bet they're paying taxes!

Green Table—Letter 8
March 11, 1994

Hey, Laura,

Mesa Verde in the Colorado Mountains was on my list of National Parks to see. Mesa Verde National Park was definitely worth the up-up-and-away trip, it was very cool! It seemed as though I drove straight up for miles and then wound around the mountains up toward the heavens—it was as cold as it was high. I recommend that you see this very impressive site! First, I was a little hesitant, because Mesa Verde is all about cliff dwellings, and I wasn't that impressed with Bandelier.

Ancient civilizations built these caves way up in the sides of mountains as a way to survive the elements and to avoid attacks from warring tribes and predators. Can you imagine these people had to live way up in the sheer face of a mountainside to survive? It just goes to show you what people are capable of when faced with adversity—a Bunker Mentality. Only the fittest will survive, and the weak will be swept away with the wind and the rain.

After Mesa Verde, I drove down into Arizona through Monument Valley and the Navajo Nation. Sadly, when I passed through, it was too dark to take pictures or even see the lay of the land. My timing was off, and it was unfortunate. I dealt with the disappointment of missing the places I read so much about because I knew I would be back some day to capture them.

I planned to stay at the hostel in Tuba City, which was on the way to Phoenix, but when I got there, I just couldn't stay there. The hostel consisted of a hundred beds lying next to each other in a school gym. It reminded me of a hospital ward in an old war movie. So, I drove a little farther to Flagstaff, Arizona and I'm staying in a hotel for $17; pretty damn good if I do say so myself!

    I called my cousin Allen, who lives in Phoenix or, as I found out, Tempe, which is pronounced *tem pee*, and I will be staying with him and his wife, Jane, for a couple of days. Allen gave me scenic directions to follow down the state. He said his path would take a little longer, but it was well worth the extra time.

    I hope you like the latest picture.

    I miss you, of course, and your spirit is with me everyday.

    Love,
    Nick
    -FeenX

Green Table

March 1994
Saguaro cacti, Arizona

Hello, Cacti!

—FeenX

Road Recipe

Lentil Soup—Have your kids sort the lentils! Wash Hands! (The first recipe ever taught to me by Aunt Lilly)

Ingredients:
- Chicken and beef stock
- Carrots
- Onions
- Garlic
- Celery
- Lentils
- Salt and white pepper to taste
- Olive oil
- Ham hock
- Ditalini

Directions:
1. Combine all ingredients and reduce by half.
2. Pull cooked ham hock from bones and chop and reserve, toss bones
3. Hand blend 1/2 of the soup until smooth and then mix with the other half.
4. Boil ditalini in chicken stock, cook until al dente, strain.
5. Add ditalini and chopped ham hock to cooked soup.
6. Serve with grated Parmesan (optional)

Suggested:

Cocktail: Harveys Bristol Cream Sherry

Wine: Pinot Noir

Beer: Sam Adams Boston Lager

Music: Background noise from the 7 o'clock CBS news from the early '70s

Chapter 12

FeenX

Audio Journal from the Car

March 12, 1994
Mood: Rising

9:45 a.m.
This definitely is Indian country—the stink of Custer is in the air. I'm worried like somehow I'm in a Cowboy and Indian movie. I'm about to drive right through the Apaches or the Navajo and the cavalry coming across the plain. I'm going to get whacked right here in the middle!

Oh, look: an Indian casino way out here. Humph. What a surprise! Can you say: loophole for the gamblers! Can you say: Tax-free loophole for the Indians! Can you say: Fuck! These Indian tribes are making billions of tax-free dollars. It's time for that law to change. Or collect a toll going in and coming out of the casino. Everybody needs to pay his or her fair share!

Cutting Crew "(I Just) Died in Your Arms" is on the radio.

> *"It must've been some kind of kiss*
> *I should've walked away, I should've walked away"*

I see some jutted mountains, they just like popped out of nowhere!

Beautiful area I'm driving through right now off of 160. It's currently 4:50 p.m. and the sun is coming down. There are just rolling hills or little mountains or something. The way the sun is hitting them they almost look like sand dunes. Like rough sand dunes, rough like the sand dunes have hair on them.

I was just in the Ute Indian reservation—very beautiful country to drive through at this time of the day, although I'm driving into the blinding sun.

I'm driving through Four Corners right now, where, ah, Welcome to the Navajo Nation, I'm in the Navajo Nation right now. Unbelievable! Four Corners is where Utah, Arizona, New Mexico, and Colorado all meet in one corner.

I'm now being welcomed into Arizona. One of the mountains looks like a big butt. I'm now leaving Big Butte National Park. Huh…

Da-da, dumpada, dumpada, bump-a-dada! A sign I just passed that said, "Watch out for animals crossing the road for the next 157 miles."

So amazing that I left snow country and I'm in the desert again. It is just so pretty you can't take your eyes off anything—it's not boring at all! Mountains, clouds, sun, uh… Unbelievable, just no way to describe it. Hopefully my picture will, I don't know, describe it better than I ever could.

Once again I'm on the long trek—poor planning! Poor plan. Wrong time of the day! Now, I won't get to see Monument Valley—and from what I saw it was GORGEOUS. Goddamn it!

I just saw two interesting signs on the road again. One said, "Watch out for water on the road." The other one said, "Don't proceed if the road is flooded." Like, would you really proceed if the road were flooded? I guess some dumb schmucks did—otherwise there wouldn't be the need for the sign.

I don't know if I expressed my frustration—I was in the midst of Monument Valley, something I desperately wanted to see, but there is no place to stay. And the closest place to stay is too far away to go and come back tomorrow. I might have to wait until I go back to Utah and Colorado. It sucks, but what are you going to do?

I swear that every car that passes is a truck, a pickup—some kind of truck.

I like this song. *"I am your lady, and you are my man."* Celine Dion, I think or that bitch Barbara Streisand, sings it. I'm not sure but I like it. It's pretty good. Maybe it's not Barbara Streisand, it's pretty good, I don't know, what do you think?

Celine Dion "The Power of Love" is on the radio.

> *"Cause I am your lady*
> *And you are my man*
> *Whenever you reach for me*
> *I'll do all that I can"*

9:10 p.m.

I don't know what my problem is but I'm very anxious about staying in a hostel right now. There was a hostel in Tuba City, the kind where a hundred cots are lined up so close they're touching each other, in a gymnasium. It was like a hospital ward or a military base they depict in old movies. Didn't even look like many people were staying there, but… I just don't want to do it. I wanted to talk to Gabby, but it's after 11 p.m. in New York and I can't even call. So now

I'm 72 miles away, it's already after 9 p.m. I'm on my way to Flagstaff, I don't know, man, I'm freaking out! I shouldn't be, but I am.

The predominant population in all these towns is American Indian. It seems like every person here is an Indian. I haven't seen one other pale face besides my own mug in the rearview mirror for miles. I feel like I'm in an episode of *Northern Exposure*. I just stopped for gas, and the lady clerk reminded me of the receptionist for the Jewish doctor.

Uh, fuck! I broke down and went to McDonald's! Got a stinking Quarter Pounder!

Elton John and Bernie Taupin "I Don't Wanna Go On With You Like That" is on the radio. *"I don't want to be a feather in your cap…"*

The stars are spectacular. Just like the entire sky is jam-packed with stars, like there isn't any more room. I don't know if it's because the land is so flat and there is more sky to see or that there isn't any city lights to brighten anything.

I should write a letter to McDonald's and tell them that I've stopped at McDonald's all over the country, fifty million McDonald's, and the one thing I can always count on is consistency. But their consistency is actually consistent all around the country. Maybe I could get a job, quality control at McDonald's. I'm sure they already have people who do that, but…

I'm on the verge of another awesome moon. It's like an evil moon—dark orange, it's huge!

Saved by the radar detector again!

I'm on this road, I talked to Allen this morning, I went to Slip Rock, really spectacular. These are places you would never know about, not in books—you stumble upon them on your way. Since I'm not in a rush, I can go any which way

I want—the long way… I just stopped on the road for a minute more, like fifteen minutes, just hanging out. Nice weather, a breeze blowing through the car. Just looking at my books. It's phenomenal not to be in a rush. In a way, photography, uh, eliminates the rush because it freezes that moment in time forever. You can take as much time and look at it as many ways as you like. That's what's cool about it—I guess, only if you can express through your photographs what you intended.

FeenX—Letter 9
March 22, 1994

Hi, Laura,
How are you? I hope you are doing well.
The scenic roads down from Colorado through Arizona were exceptional! I drove through Red Rock country and Sedona—it was fucking beautiful! The red mountains, green forests, blue skies, and fresh air were remarkable! I traveled around the North Rim of the Grand Canyon, which was closed by winter, to Flagstaff, which had many cool brew pubs in a "granola munching" atmosphere, to Phoenix, my resting destination. By the time I got to Phoenix, it was probably 50 degrees warmer than when I drove past the Grand Canyon, only six hours earlier—Simply amazing!

Actual saguaro (pronounced sa-war-oh) cactus littered the mountainsides like weeds—they look like forks standing on their stem. I couldn't tell whether they were waving hello or goodnight to me as the sun was setting, but it was a spectacular sight. I got to my cousin's around 8 p.m., and it was so warm that I had to change into shorts immediately. To give you an idea how warm it was, people were wearing shorts and still sweating. It wasn't even officially spring yet!

As soon as I walked through their door, Jane, my cousin's wife, threw her arms around me to welcome me into their home. Jane squeezed me so tightly it caught me by surprise. I thought it was a surprising welcome because I have only spoken with her briefly a couple of times at an occasional family gathering. It was a major welcoming, and it did feel good. In the back of my mind, I got the feeling that she was missing something, home or family, anyone's home or family.

Nobody had traveled out that far from back East to see them. It was like a "Star Trek" episode where someone visited Pluto from Earth after a thousand years. Anyway, it made me feel good. Jane practically begged me to stay with them for as long as I liked. They had a bedroom for me to stay and everything.

I talked it over with Allen. He assured me it was fine, and he even thought he might be able to find me some temporary work.

I thought it was an unbelievable opportunity to have fall into my lap. I had a home base in Phoenix relatively close to some of the greatest sites to be photographed in the country, and I could be with family all at the same time.

I had planned on staying for just the weekend, then because of the generous offer I thought I'd be staying for a week, but two weeks have passed and there is no departure date in sight. My cousin and his wife have been so kind to me. Every step of this journey surprises me. The hospitality I'm experiencing has been amazing! It's obviously beneficial for me to accept these offers, but I wonder if it also benefits the gracious hosts in some way. Everyone seems as excited to see me as I am to see them. Maybe it's because my trip reminds the people who have moved far away from their home of their own journey, and of the past they left behind—just a guess.

To give you some insight of the new world that I'm currently living in, I give you the first episode of a brand new, made-for-TV series: Nick Anthony—Marriage Counselor.

Allen and Jane have an interesting relationship. Interesting probably isn't the right word. "Tense," that's it, tense is definitely the right word. There always seems to be this tension between them that I can't figure out. I feel that my presence here is a good thing, a needed thing. Without me or some other distraction giving them some space, there would be some breaking. I'm like a referee of sorts. I don't go in and break up the action, but just by being there I provide the necessary buffer and restraint.

Jane is a year or two younger than I and appears to be a high-maintenance blonde from Michigan, or she used to be. I think she is bored and tired of living in this very young college town. She makes it sound as if Allen dragged her out here so he could go back to school for the past four years, but I know that not to be the case.

Allen, on the other hand, is a couple of years older than me and is the active outdoorsman type—mountain biking, hiking, camping, a-going-to-the-gym-everyday guy and he always has been. The young college town with its mountains and landscape lends itself to his active lifestyle. Jane wants nothing to do with it.

Allen throws all this guilt her way, because she isn't the slightest bit interested in getting involved. He does it in a passive-aggressive way that I'm sure can be quite annoying, and I'm sure he doesn't even realize what he's doing. I'm also sure that I've been guilty of this crime myself. I think it is an Italian or Jewish family thing. Being able to watch from the outside really shows how harmful the guilt, in its most hideous form, can be to a relationship. Sometimes, you need to be on the outside to understand and see how destructive the effects can be. I'm sure he doesn't see it at all.

Allen will drop comments that Jane won't go to the gym and work out with him, or she won't go on mountain bike rides, or play tennis, or go on a hike, or my favorite—"She's eating too much of the wrong thing." Jane gets really pissed off because she doesn't want to hear it and Allen backs off with, "never mind," as though that's supposed to take all of his hen pecking back. I'm sure Allen thinks his comments are no big deal, but he never lets anything go, and he always has to get his digs in. I know that feeling and, again, I've been both the giver and receiver of this crime. I've felt his frustration, and I know why he feels the need to drop the comments and that's a problem.

Allen does many things by himself and with his faithful companion, the puppy named Kobe, who doesn't listen to anything anyone says. Allen feels that Jane should be sharing life and times with him, as most people do with their spouse.

When they do things together, it usually involves other people. There is always someone else around. Whether it was me or one of their many graduate school friends, Jane and Allen are never alone. Kobe acts like the child they don't have. At times, I think, his dog really is his best friend. Stay tuned for future episodes of Nick Anthony—Marriage Counselor.

I'm waiting for some new pictures to come back from the lab. I can't wait! I'm also planning a couple of photo safaris soon! I'll let you know how they turn out.

Everything has been great, except walking Kobe and picking up his shit. How fucked up is that? I'm supposedly higher up on the chain of beasts, but this dog is walking me around the block while I'm picking up his shit in a plastic bag. I need to rethink the value of intelligence a little bit.

I hope you like the latest picture. I hope this letter finds you well.

        Life is amazing! Love you!
        Nick
        -FeenX

March 1994
Sedona, Arizona

Cathedral Rock
—FeenX

Chapter 13

Tempe Tempe Tempe

Audio Journal from the Car

March 24, 1994
Mood: Free falling

2:30 p.m.
Just passed a trout farm—cool little rapidy-type river, which reminds me of *A River Runs Through It.* Oh, I like this combination, what do you think about it? A road less traveled and a river runs through it. Or maybe this: *A River Runs Through a Road Less Traveled.* The river that runs through a road less traveled… Huh. I stumbled upon the river that runs through a road less traveled. Hahahaha, I like it!

2:45 p.m.
Go and get yaself to the Grand Canyon, whatcha waitin' for? "Get yaself to the Grand Canyon."—Danny Glover in the *Grand Canyon*.

2:50 p.m.
I feel like I've been to the Grand Canyon already with all these mountains and peaks and rivers and valleys. And I haven't even gotten there yet…

3:45 p.m.
I'm driving through—I suspect—I'm driving through Sedona right now, it's, uh, if I said R E D everywhere, I wouldn't be lying. I can't

believe that Sedona isn't a National Park… What does it take?

    I bet it gets hot as balls out here in summertime! It's already hot here—in March!

    The Eagles "New Kid in Town" is on the radio. *"Everybody loves him. He's holdin' her."* This song always brings me back to *"The Year of the Cat,"* which reminds me of when I was twelve. I was in love with Denise Macallan who was fourteen. We did everything together. Everything that twelve and fourteen-year-old kids did back in my day: skateboarding, walking for miles around the neighborhood, endlessly talking and lying in the grass staring up at the sky, enjoying life, hanging out, and then—Danny Lupo enters the picture. Danny-fucking-Lupo! The name Danny still annoys the hell out of me to this day! I should explain a little bit… She was my first love—crush, whatever and then the new kid moves into the neighborhood… I'll just leave it there. Listen to the song it explains it…

    Eagle's lyrics: "New Kid in Town" is on the radio.

> *"Johnny-come-lately, the new kid in town,*
> *Everybody loves you, so don't let them down."*

    Anyway, this town I'm driving through, Sedona, Arizona. Phenomenal! Little shops, restaurants, and scenery that's not from this world! Red rock everywhere like Mars. Spectacular scenery—explosions of red monolith striped with thin lines of green ending before pluming up into the crisp blue heavens. I realize what the difference is between great photographers and snapshot artists clicking away. I waited in one place for a couple of hours for the right light, angle, composition, and for these freaken people to get out of my frame. I don't care how many people are clicking away; I don't care how good the equipment looks, or how expensive it is—it's the patience and getting the right picture, *the perfect bite.*

There just aren't words to describe the beauty I'm in the middle of—I feel overwhelmed by emotion. You just have to see it to believe it.

Today I met, believe it or not, Dick and Jane from Grand Rapids, Michigan. I introduced myself and talked to them a bit about their travels and bumped into them again at a different site. It was funny, I was waiting at that one Citadel Rock spot for what seemed to me a hundred years and a day and they were talking to me there. Then I went to this Chapel Hill and all of a sudden they walked in on me, capturing… Funny, they were the first people I ran into and didn't tell my whole life story to.

Radar detector just started blinking, telling me I only have ten hours left before it stops working.

Phoenix!

Cool! I just saw my first big cactus! Cool, baby!

Steve Miller "Jungle Love" is on the radio.

> *"… it's driving me mad*
> *It's making me crazy"*

Now I see a whole bunch of cacti. It's too bad there isn't light out to take some pictures. Not enough light, anyway. The cacti are everywhere—like weeds!

I just saw an orange tree growing by itself on the side of the road in a residential area—it's cool!

Just saw a place called Rent-a-Vet! You can just rent a Corvette. Pretty cool, huh?

This should be my theme song: *"My skin began to turn red. Been through the desert on a horse with no name."* Is it Glen Campbell? America? *"It felt good to be out of the rain..."*
America "A Horse with No Name" is on the radio."

> *"...It felt good to be out of the rain*
> *In the desert you can remember your name*
> *'Cause there ain't no one for to give you no pain"*

March 26, 1994
Mood: No pride and loving life
1:30 p.m.
Oh, I got another job today in Phoenix…
I'm one crazy motherfucker, man! Hahahaha! Now I have to call to quit my other job because I just got a fucking pizza delivery job for Domino's Pizza, baby! Who's fucking slicker than I am? Not too many people. Hahahahahaha. It had to be the most ridiculous interview I've ever had, I fill out the application, talk to the lady, I mean she asked if I had a driver's license. Before you know it, she's calling in my paperwork and saying, "I guess you're hired." She's laughing as much as I am!

Tip: Remember that the next time you let the pizza guy in—they hire anybody!

This pizza gig, the whole thing is just classic. Too funny! I just went in, the manager, I guess, looks at my papers, doesn't look at my car or anything. He's like, "You need to take a Domino's driving class and then we'll have you drive with someone for an hour."

Tomorrow, bing-ita-bang-ita-boom I drive on my own. Fabulous, isn't it?

Now it's official—I'm Mr. Pizza Guy from *Fast Times at Ridgemont High*! Or, maybe I could be like the Extra Anchovies Please Pizza Guy from that other movie—wouldn't that be a sweet deal? Schweet!

Note from N.Y.:

Paul and Jack called at 5:30 a.m. N.Y. time, 2:30 a.m. my time. And ah, they were calling me to tell me Richard's bachelor party was a success. Paul was completely out of his mind. Richard jumped out of the hot seat; Jack shouldered the brunt of it all. Which isn't too surprising and then he proceeded to pass out while he was on the phone with me. They had to leave in three hours for Costa Rica as a continuation of the party. Man, I wish I were with them!

Tempe Tempe Tempe—Letter 10
April 3, 1994

Hey, Laura,

How's it going? I hope all is well with you.

Life in old AZ is cool, well, it's hot, but I mean besides the temperature—it's been cool. Allen and Jane have access to a pool and Jacuzzi at their condo complex, which makes it more than tolerable. Not bad when you consider the time of the year and the ridiculous weather you've been having back East. Piña Coladas by the Jacuzzi after work is choice, and if you have the means, I highly recommend it.

More observations about my new atmosphere: the city of Tempe, and for that matter, Phoenix, Mesa, Scottsdale, and Camelback, are all set up in neat, well-organized grids. All the houses are stacked right next to each other, and there is all this spacious land left to itself. One sandbox is set right next to the next sandbox. All the streets run parallel or perpendicular to each other so it's easy to find your way around, but it's a bit "cookie cutter" if you know what I mean. Nobody has a lawn because of the blazing sun, but they have found creative ways to paint cement and to use rocks and desert plants to decorate their square of land.

Will you look at what time it is? Are you ready for another episode of Nick Anthony—Marriage Counselor?

It's interesting coexisting with other people in their little jungle habitat. I've been trying to help out here and there—a little cooking, a little babysitting this damn dog, and a little story telling.

I noticed that my cousin takes on most of the responsibilities of the household. Allen does all the shopping, most of the cooking, takes care of the dog, changes the oil in the car, etc. While Jane's day job is more flexible and demands less of her time than his, Allen pulls his weight plus most of her weight, yet she still pulls most of the strings.

Jane plays helpless when it's convenient and plays the walking boss when she knows she can get away with it, which is most of the time. Allen would eat a bowl of worms if she asked him to. Again, I'm not saying that my cousin is a sap; it's just easier for me to see this from the outside.

Jane has whipped him quite a bit, and maybe he holds on too tightly—it's probably a bit of both. Allen wants to make everything okay, and he tries to prevent any problems by just doing whatever Jane asks him to do. I know it bothers him because you can see the shakes of his head or huffs under his breath, and he always drops the comments, then finishes with, "never mind."

Allen definitely holds on too tightly. He needs to relax, go with the punches. He should do the things that he wants and let Jane do the things she wants without putting any pressure on her. Maybe if that happened, the tension would go away. Maybe, if she pulled some of the weight, he would feel less animosity or resentment and drop fewer comments.

When it comes down to it, Allen and Jane just don't enjoy the same things. I can't figure out if he changed in some way for her or she changed in some way for him, or maybe each changed for each other. I do know that when you change for someone or try to change someone else, the old self will always resurface because our essence can't be changed permanently. Resentment usually follows. Either you resent the person trying to change you or the other person resents the fact that you are trying to change them. There is the other hand, where you try to change yourself for someone else, and then you resent yourself for being an idiot and you resent the other person because they were the reason you changed in the first place.

My cousin had to know the woman he was marrying, didn't he? I think, maybe, he just wanted so badly to be in love, he overlooked everything he should have been paying attention to. Wanting and overlooking—something we all have done at times about one thing or another. They're two of the reasons why there is so much failure in daily life; the reasons businesses fail so often. Wanting and overlooking are two of the biggest reasons that the divorce rate is so high.

Allen just doesn't see that he made a mistake. In his mind, Jane is the girl that would marry him and, without her, he would be alone in the world. For Allen, nothing is worse than being alone. He married his first girlfriend and that very rarely works out. Enough of Nick Anthony—Marriage Counselor Change the channel!

Some interesting developments have come up during my time here in AZ. I've needed to make some money to pay for some of the bills that seem to keep piling up, out of nowhere. Yes, I had to get a job. Can you imagine the horror? "Oh, the horror. The horror..."

Let's go down the list:

I started the training process as a waiter at some full-service chain restaurant. I got to be the idiot employee who plays all the games with management, interesting switch, huh? That process didn't last too long, because I got a better offer from Domino's Pizza—chauffeuring pizza around town. How's that for a kick? I think it's pretty funny. My first delivery took one and a half hours. I was driving around like a mental patient trying to find this place in an apartment complex the size of an airport.

Can you say free pizza; can you say no tip????

The customers could say it, and they did to my face!

The next job after the Domino's job was as a waiter in a small Italian restaurant, which is where I am now, and it's going really well—none of the political bullshit that's in the corporate environment. I iron my shirt before I go to work, I get my station organized before I start to take orders, collect money, clean up, and go home. It's mindless. I can just go to work, do a job, and bring nothing but money home. I've also met many interesting people—both coworkers and customers. The customers start talking with me—asking me about life and death, and before you know it, they are inviting me to visit them if, while roaming around, I'm ever in their neck of the woods. How cool is that?

Along with the restaurant gig, I occasionally sell beer by the bucket at baseball spring training games and Indy car races. "Beer here, get your ice-cold beer!!!" It's so loud at the car races that everyone has to wear earplugs. Communication is the obvious problem because of these damn earplugs. The challenge is to get people's attention while they are waiting for a car crash. So, I have found that if you just fly the can in the air, people do respond. The money is all-good and it's all cash.

A funny observation: The people that go to the car races are only interested in two things—car crashes (which is what brings people to the races in the first place—let's be honest) and their beer, which is the only way to tolerate sitting in 110-degree sun to wait for car crashes.

Mind you, they aren't interested in good-quality beer, in my opinion, they just want their beer. They like their Bud, their Coors, their MGD, and such. The interesting thing is that they are picky about these beers. A Bud man can only drink Bud, and a MGD man won't drink Bud or Coors, only MGD. Until, that is, the temperature starts going up past 100 degrees, and you're sold out of their beer—then they will drink anything in a can. Everyone, including myself, is judgmental and particular in their own reality, and everything is relative. Someone who drinks Sierra Nevada looks down at the person who drinks Budweiser, yet the person who drinks Bud looks down at the person drinking Coors Light. Meanwhile, we will all drink piss if there is nothing else to drink. Human nature, I guess.

Another easy example of what people are particular about is their coffee house choices. "Oh, I can't drink XYZ's coffee, their coffee is awful, I only drink coffee from the beans that Juan Valdez himself has picked." Little do they know he picked his nose and his ass with the same fingers—there's no board of health regulations in those countries! Think about it!

I know these jobs must seem pretty foolish or silly to you, but doing what you have to do to survive is a humbling, growing experience—not to mention very necessary and rewarding—look at all these stories I have to tell.

> I hope you like the latest picture.
> I wonder how you are doing.
> All my love,
> Nick
>
> -FeenX

April 1994
Grand Canyon, Arizona

Damsel's Tower
—FeenX

Road Recipe

Spaghetti and Meatballs with Tomato Sauce—Figure out what 2 bunch is and you might have a chance! (Grandma...)

Ingredients / Sauce:

Large onion brunoise	Fennel Seed
Fresh garlic chopped	Black pepper and kosher salt
Basil	Beef stock
Olive oil	Plum tomatoes
Sugar	Grated Parmesan
	Butter

Directions / Sauce:

1. Sauté: olive oil, Large onion brunoise, fresh garlic chopped, until golden
2. Then add: fennel seed, basil, black pepper and kosher salt, plum tomatoes, and beef stock
3. Simmer: for 25 minutes
4. Blend: with hand blender until smooth
5. Then add: sugar and simmer for 5 minutes
6. Boil lots of salted water, add spaghetti cook until al dente and drain.
7. Toss with spaghetti and grated parmesan and butter
8. Add: Meatballs

Ingredients / Meatballs:

Pork	Eggs
Beef	Salt and pepper
	Onion Powder
Grated cheese	Parsley
Breadcrumbs	Garlic

Directions Meatballs:

1. Mix: all ingredients,
2. Shape and bake: balls, 400-degree oven.
3. Add and simmer: to tomato sauce for 5 minutes

Suggestions:

Cocktail: Champagne Cocktail
Wine: Full-bodied—Cabernet Sauvignon or Chianti
Beer: Golden Pale Ale
Music: "Stornelli Amorisi" by Claudio Villa

Chapter 14

The Road

Audio Journal from the Car

April 6, 1994
Mood: Loving life

10:30 a.m.
Grammy's B-day today! Happy Birthday, Grammy!

There are some really crazy rules in Arizona. Like, how about, you can wear side arms. More to the point, you must display guns when you carry them—No concealing them! The Harley-motorcycle guy I'm driving next to right now as you can hear (motorcycle noise): He's got shotgun shells hanging in bands across his chest and a shot gun slung in a holster on the motorcycle…I'm not making this shit up!

Pearl Jam "Even Flow" is on the radio.

> *"… Thoughts arrive like butterflies*
> *Oh, he don't know, so he chases them away, yeah…ooh…*
> *Oh, someday yet, he'll begin his life again…life again…life again…"*

Once again, a wave of Laura is crashing in on me, I think about her and then I don't… I just heard her say, "I'm going to make some snickity snackities! Yeah!" And, thinking of picking up a six pack of some obscure beer we've never had and enjoying it with her…

♦ ☆ ✸

April 8, 1994
Mood: Late night and drunk
1:00 a.m.

Pretty scary tonight, baaaaaybee! A beautiful girl was my waitress tonight, baaaaaybee! Her name was Jenny and she was giving me the vibe. And, what did Nick do? Did Nick sulk in his beer and sit there like a putz? No, he came through, he engaged. Because she was into different brews, which is very odd for a girl, he said, maybe in not so many words,

"Hey, baaaaaybee, I know of a place that serves 228 beers in Scottsdale."

"I know where that is," she said, "but I've never been there."

I said, "Well, maybe we could go there together sometime."

And she said, "I have a boyfriend" and turned completely red in the face.

"Maybe he wouldn't be too happy if we went to the beer place."

"I think you're right," she said, "but he doesn't own me, I work on the weekends, it would have to be during the week. Make sure you come back to see me."

So, it was fun, while fantasizing. The flirtation, the smile, the smile, ah the back and forth. Ah... she was sweet, tall, blonde hair, short blonde hair, very short. Very nice legs—they were what I was attracted to from the get go... Oh, wasn't that a Mustang showing off! Oh, she was sweet Jenny, Jen, Jen, maybe I will go back and see her—escalate things a scoochie. Jenny, Jen, beautiful smile, Jen. Unbelievable!

Wowie! The Fuzz just fucking blew by me! Who said this? "If it ain't the mighty whitey. The Fuzz." —someone from a *Dirty Harry* movie.

Written Journal Entry

April 11, 1994

Unexpected Surprise

    Funny, this whole time, I've been driving, philosophizing, cooking, learning, seeing America, making pictures, growing, and ultimately trying to figure it all out. I don't think it's possible to figure it all out, but I'm a daydream believer. I was on a photo safari hunting for something great, something new, looking to bag the elephant.

    I drove up to the edge and, all of a sudden, there she was standing right front of me, and she was beautiful. Not a classic beauty per se but simply amazing nonetheless. It seemed that she changed with each movement of the sun. There was something about the way the sun moved around her that changed the color of her hair, the freckles on her face, and the glistening of her eyes.

    She told me her sad tale and I truly listened to each word, looking deeply into her eyes, somehow trying to absorb her pain. She told me about the violent times that I just couldn't imagine, but I could see the subtle scars, and they weren't all physical. You could tell that time played a significant factor. The person she was managed to find a way to shine through—that couldn't be taken away.

    I listened all day, just sitting by the edge, watching the changes that the sun brought to her. I wondered at times if I were dreaming. She didn't want to go home yet so I said we could go back to my humble roadside motel. I had a bottle of Goslings rum that I picked up somewhere along the way. I didn't take any pictures that day except for the pictures in my mind. I never even pulled out my camera. I knew I should be writing everything that happened in my journal. But, she was so fragile at that moment.

    I turned on the radio. We stood close holding each other's hands in the middle of the room looking into each other's eyes. The music played in the background, but we slowly swayed back and forth as if there wasn't any music at all. We slow danced and with each move to the right or left her head would sway following our movement with a slight delay. She looked deeply into my eyes and I couldn't release my eyes as hard as I tried. Then she smiled gently as her eyes welled up—but not enough to release a tear. She put her head into my shoulder and I stroked her hair that smelled so sweet as I closed my eyes and savored the moment. As I opened my eyes and tried to bring comfort to someone who truly needed to be held—she melted in my arms. I closed my eyes again and we fused together. This time when I opened my eyes, she was gone.

    I've been back to that edge many times hoping I might see her, but I've never seen her again. Except for the smell of her skin and the burned imprint in my mind, she was gone forever.

The Road—Letter 11
April 20, 1994

Hi, Laura,

I'm wondering how you're doing. I'm fine.

When I've had time off from work, I've gone on numerous, what I like to call, "photo safaris." On one occasion, I had the company of my new buddy Daniel. He went to graduate school with my cousin and has become a good friend of mine through the association. He also fancies himself to be a photo enthusiast. He's originally from Long Island—how's that for a small world? I might have driven past him on the Long Island Expressway at one time or another and not even have known it. I felt a little safer to be traveling through the unknown with someone else. At times, traveling alone could be intimidating, especially camping in the wilderness at night. It's also nice to have someone talk back to you; I can only tolerate talking to myself for so long. Importantly, Daniel, a fellow photographer, understands the patience required when the hunt is on—so he is not burdensome.

Generally, when I go on safari, I hunt and explore for pictures by myself. There's a certain tranquility and peace in the quiet of my mind that is understood and appreciated only when I'm alone. It's funny because it lives there all the time; I just never knew it. When I go on safari, I usually drive as far as my car and body will take and return me safely.

I took many, many trips to the Grand Canyon—glorious sunsets turning the flat landscape into a spectacular three-dimensional wonderland. The sunrises were so peaceful. When the sun would wake up, the dewy mist would rise from the canyon floor and float up over your head right before your eyes. AMAZING GRACE!

Nature puts on a show that's never a disappointment. Maybe it was the angle or the cloud formations, or the colors of rock, sky, or flowers, but every minute was astounding and different.

Sedona, known for its rich, red rock formations, was very impressive. I would like to go back sometime when there is white snow painted on the red mountains. I can only imagine how incredible it would be.

Canyon de Chelly—pronounced canyon dee-shay, not *shelly* as I was corrected, was worth every, out-of-the-way minute getting there—and it was way out of the way!

Flagstaff was basically the midway point between Phoenix and the National Parks. You either had to drive through it or stop there to rest in order to get anywhere.

Monument Valley—can you say super-fine red sand everywhere? Can you say super spectacular! Monument Valley is considered Four Corners country. Four Corners is the only place in the entire United States where four states (Utah, Colorado, Arizona, and New Mexico) touch in the same spot—I knew I would be back! Monument Valley is not a National Park, as many people think. It is actually an Indian reservation. Most western movies use Monument Valley as their backdrop.

I spent ten glorious days in Utah, which is possibly the most beautiful state the country has to offer. I went to Bryce Canyon National Park, which is different from anything you've ever seen on earth. I thought I had landed on another planet.

The Road

Moab, Utah is all about huge mammoth rocks and rock formations. Moab, sounds like something out of the Bible, and it is where serious mountain bikers go to bunny hop and have a blast.

The Arches National Park, just north of Moab, is the *reason* people climb to the top. When I started to climb the mountain, it was 95 degrees at the base and, when I got to the top, there was snow around this massive arch. The arch is so large that you can look through it from a distance and see snow-covered mountains with piercing blue skies dusted with these puffy white clouds. I sweated my ass off lugging my cameras, tripods, and winter gear up the steep mountain, but it was well worth the price when I got to the frozen top.

Zion National Park—beautiful and tranquil.

Canyonlands National Park—EXPANSIVE!

Dead Horse Point is a state park, not a National Park so you do not salute it, but you should stop and pay it homage because God did a fabulous job creating it. You could easily drive by without even knowing it was there, which would definitely be a sin.

I camped and *hosteled* all the way. When I camped, I had my trusty cleaver to protect me. Advice: If you are going to protect yourself with your favorite weapon of choice, know how to use it, and be prepared to be victorious or don't even bring it out. Remember, there is nothing worse than getting chopped up with your own weapon. I have to be careful.

Did you know that you could set up camp in any national forest as long as you are a hundred feet off the highway? Sometimes I felt uneasy about camping out in the wilderness—like I was in a scene out of *Deliverance* with Ned Beatty squealing like a pig or something. I could convince myself that toothless inbreds were just waiting for me to pull my car over so they could make me squeal like a pig. I told you I have a bit of an imagination. If I scared myself too much, I'd just squeeze into my sleeping bag right there in the car and lock up.

There were times on some of my longer trips that I didn't shave, and my hair was way out of control. I would walk into a civilized area after being out in the "bush" for days and people would be eyeballing me, treating me like a bum. For example, I walked into this diner that was actually a trailer that had only one row of seats at the counter. The cook smoked while he cooked, and the waitress smoked while she waited, and the customers smoked while they ate. I tried to breathe as I dusted off and observed my new environment.

I could see people whispering to each other, wondering who this stranger was invading their town. The thought that I was being judged completely on my appearance pissed me off! They didn't know who I was or what I was doing. Yet, I was looked upon and whispered about as this bad-guy stranger who came into their town. Their fucking town! I'm the fucking bad-guy stranger!? I would just keep to myself, laugh at first, and then get angry.

Judging people by their appearance has become the national pastime, like baseball and apple pie. I guess we all do a bit of judging to some extent. It's the old "book by the cover" adage. When you're the one being gossiped about, it puts the shoe on the other foot. It's disturbing to me, and something I'm sure I've been guilty of in my past, which I want to work on in the future.

The Road

This country has so much to offer and these national treasures aren't being appreciated by the masses. I would guess that there are more people from other countries at these glorious places than U.S. citizens. Is Disney World really better than all this natural beauty???

Sometimes I forget that this is the good old U.S.A. where the almighty dollar rules! Sometimes I just want to hide myself in the woods far away from our backward society. Money, money, money! Teachers who educate our future, and police and firemen who risk their lives to make our lives safe get paid little in our upside-down world. While changing dollars in the stock markets, being a lawyer and manipulating both sides of the system, or preying on people's weaknesses as insurance salesmen do, is hidden by honorable job titles and large paychecks, making the few very rich. I'm telling you, the abyss between the haves and have-nots in this country is getting greater and greater. The inequity can't continue like this forever and won't. If nothing changes, I predict there will be some type of major rebellion or revolution in our lifetime.

Sorry, I guess I went off on a small tangent. WOW, I finally got to use the word "tangent," and I thought I would never be able to use what I learned in that math class.

Back to the heat factor in good old Tempe, AZ: It can get pretty hot here, and from what I'm told, it's not even the hot season yet. People keep saying:

"Well, at least it's dry heat."

"Well, it's not as bad as it being hot, hazy, and humid like back East."

Well, I say, ha! You hear me? Ha! Ha! What a laugh, 110 degrees is 110 degrees!

You don't sweat here because it evaporates instantly. Basically, you're in a convection oven—baking as opposed to sweating in a sauna. Personally, if I'm sweating, I would like to know I'm sweating. In AZ, a lot of people walk around dehydrated with salt deposits all over them. It's not a pretty sight, I'll tell you that.

And, now for another episode in the continuing saga of Nick Anthony—(Lunatic) Marriage Counselor.

I think my cousin thinks that it's his job to make his wife happy, and I believe he thinks it's her job to make him happy. This notion is one of the biggest misconceptions about healthy relationships on the planet. If there is one thing I've realized here on the road it's that it's no one's responsibility to be the keeper of someone else's happiness. The only reasonable thing anyone can do for any relationship they're a part of is find true happiness within himself or herself. After all, that is where true happiness is; the other kind of happiness is fleeting and dependent upon other uncontrollable factors. No one can maintain perfection, and no one should be responsible for another person's happiness.

I'm not saying that you can't make someone happy. I'm saying that it isn't possible or fair to expect or to be expected to control and maintain someone else's inner happiness. You need to find happiness within yourself before you can share it with others.

If you can be happy and comfortable with yourself, and if you can find someone who is happy and comfortable with himself or herself, you truly have something special and a strong foundation to build a solid relationship on. If you're depending on someone to make you happy, or someone is depending on you to make them happy, you are doomed to failure because the pressure of failure is overwhelming. There will always be a letdown; it's human nature.

All that being said, somehow I know my cousin's marriage is doomed. All right then, there it is, I wrote it down. It is written; it is done. My cousin, his wife, or both will eventually come to this realization.

My conclusions from this case—I've learned:
- You can't hold on too tightly.
- You can't change for the other person—the person you are will always come back.
- You can't change the other person—it's not fair, and they will eventually change back.
- You don't marry your first girlfriend without dating other girls first, so you have a comparable frame of reference.
- You can't be responsible for someone else's happiness.
- Someone can't be responsible for your happiness.

—Nick Anthony—Marriage Counselor.

I'm retiring; this kind of work is too mentally exhausting. I don't know, could it be that I'm wrong about this case, maybe? Nah, For-getta-bout-it...

Don't get me wrong, Allen and Jane are great people, individually. I just don't believe they are right for each other. I must not forget to mention that Allen and Jane have been so kind and giving to me, I can't stand it! We got a chance to really get to know each other and bond—I feel so lucky!

I did forget to mention that we went to see Jimmy Buffett in concert outside at a closed Air

Force base. I know, I swore that I would never go to another outside concert since the monsoon at the Eric Clapton disaster in Saratoga, but what were the chances for rain in the desert? And besides, you have to take chances in life. It was a pretty cool experience being outside, in the desert at night, at an old abandoned Air Force base grooving to the mellow party sounds of the master relaxer—Jimmy Buffett.

    Buffett has a cult following like the Grateful Dead or something. He's like the poster child for drinking margaritas, smoking a few joints, lying back, and sailing away from everything.

    Surprisingly enough, it was at the concert, for the first time, my cousin and his wife appeared to be having a really good time together. It was nice. It doesn't change my prediction; it was just nice.

    On a separate note, I plan on coming back to the East Coast for a long weekend at the end of April. Richard and Silvia are getting married on April 30th.

    Please call me if you would like to catch up in person while I'm back home. I only plan on being home for a few days, and it would be great to see you.

    I'm happy and I'm okay with myself; I hope you are the same. I hope you will call when I'm home. I would really like to see you.

        Love,
        Nick
        -FeenX

April 1994
The Arches, Utah

*The Reason People
Climb to the Top*

—FeenX

Road Recipe

Linguini with Broccoli Rabe, Garlic, Sausage, and Cannellini Beans—Make the effort, find the broccoli rabe and cannellini beans—just do it! (A mélange of ingredients inspired at Il Boschetto on Gunhill Road in the Bronx)

Ingredients:
- Olive oil
- Fresh chopped Garlic
- Broccoli Rabe
- Sausage
- Cannelini beans
- Chicken Stock
- Crushed red pepper
- Black pepper and salt
- Grated Parmesan
- Linguini
- Butter

Directions:
1. Sauté: Olive oil, fresh chopped garlic, broccoli rabe, cannelini beans
2. Then add: crushed red pepper, black pepper and salt, chicken stock
3. Roast: sweet Italian sausage and slice on the bias.
4. Boil: linguini in lots of salted water until al dente and drain thoroughly.
5. Toss: Linguini with sautéed ingredients and butter.
6. Top with sausage and grated Parmesan.

Suggestions:
Cocktail: Vodka tonic with Lemon
Wine: Viognier, Dry Italian Rose
Beer: Tsingtao, Moretti Rosa
Music: "Boulevard of Broken Dreams" by Tony Bennett

Audio Journal from the Car

April 21, 1994
Mood: Psyched!

2:30 p.m.

Nick Anthony, now ex-pizza delivery guy. Breakin' the law, breakin' the law, I must be going too fast! I left "no shirt, shorts, lying by the pool" weather, and I'm still ninety miles away from Flagstaff and it's cold enough to put my windows up. Unbelievable!

The views are unbelievable, white-capped mountains, red rock, gorgeous!

Next twenty miles, watch for elk. Is that the coolest fucking sign or what? To make sure you don't hit an elk they have to post signs. Cool!

On the radio: They've just announced new music coming out, it's Blind Melon "No Rain." It's the song that has been on the radio for months. *All I can say is that my life is pretty plain.* That's not new Blind Melon. Are they out of their mind?!

Blind Melon "No Rain" is on the radio. I'm at Coconino National Park, looking at the San Francisco Peaks—awesome! Covered with snow—just beautiful.

Bob Seger "Old Time Rock and Roll" is on the radio.

"Just take those old records off the shelf"

Good ass music today!
Now, Cream "Strange Brew" is on the radio.

*"She's a witch of trouble in electric blue,
In her own mad mind she's in love with you."*

I should call Aunt Lilly and tell her where I... *voice cracking* am. Oh my God. It's like for a couple of seconds she was still alive. And I could have called her. I'm very sad right now… I miss Aunt Lilly, *voice cracking* I miss her a lot… I can't believe I…

✦ ☆ ✺

Took me three and a half hours to get to the Grand Canyon from Phoenix—not bad. Considering they told me it would take five, six, seven hours.

✦ ☆ ✺

April 23, 1994
Mood: Flying high!

1:45 p.m.
Incredible song! I'm in deep thought about Laura and what comes on? Chicago "Does Anyone Really Know What Time It Is?" is on the radio.

> *"As I was walking down the street one day*
> *A man came up to me and asked me what the time was that was on my watch, yeah*
> *And I said"*

If I forget to write it down: yesterday while I was making pictures of the Grand Canyon, doing my gig, I could hear people talking about me, saying wow, look that photographer is hanging off the cliff, taking pictures—cool!

There were also couples in romantic moments, as the sun set, having wine and cheese, gazing into each other's eyes. Sooo romantic. Why do I need to be reminded? I would love to be doing this with Laura. Why won't she let me in?

Goddamn! It's going to be a fucking glorious day today!

I like this remake a lot! Mariah Carey "Without You" is on the radio.

"I can't live
If living is without you"

From the movie *Scarface*:

Frank: And what happens if we don't have the buy money for Sosa? You think he's gonna send us a bill? No, he's going to send a fucking hit squad!

Tony: Okay, Frank, so I go on the street, make a deal here or there.

Frank: Oh, you go on the street?

Tony: I have ears.

Frank: Maybe you and Sosa know something I don't.

Tony: I never turned you Frank, I made what I could on the side, but I remained loyal!

Great lines!

As far as I'm concerned, you need to be at the Grand Canyon before nine o'clock a.m., or right before sunset, around 4:00 p.m., because that's the only way the hills come alive! To the sound of music! Ahhhhhahhhah!

Bob Dylan "Like a Rolling Stone" is on the radio.

"How does it feel
To be without a home
Like a complete unknown"

Chapter 15
Revelations

After reading the letters, I sat back in my seat with my seatbelt still fastened and my tray table still down. The eleventh letter was my last letter to Laura. I hadn't seen her since I gave her key back seven months before. I didn't remember exactly when we had last spoken to each other , but somewhere along the way, we had talked by phone. I had called her, of course. Somehow, Laura hadn't remembered our previous conversation. We caught up a little bit, and Laura apologized for not getting in touch for my birthday. I told her "no problem," like it wasn't a problem. I remember telling her that I missed her. I wanted Laura to know I still cared very much, so I told her that I loved her. I also remembered what I wanted her response to be and what her response had actually been.

Laura just said, "Okay, take care, keep in touch, be careful." It took her about a second and a half to rattle off the standard blowoff, "auf wiedersehen," that I was forced to get used to.

Have I told you that I've been accused of being cynical before? Maybe Laura was saying what I wanted her to say without actually saying the words. I couldn't tell anymore and that was okay, because I couldn't let her be my central focus anymore. I couldn't force her to let me in, and she had the chain on the door.

For the first time, it really started to sink in. From the first letter to the last, I realized where I had been and how far I had come. My growth could be measured, and it was all positive. Life exposed itself and its lessons to me everyday. Without intentionally looking for it, I was finding out about the meaning of life. I was gaining a clearer understanding of people and relationships. The country that I grew up in but never really saw from behind the wheel of my car in Westchester was beautiful beyond words, unbelievable and huge.

It turns out that Paul was right.

I was growing spiritually as well as mentally. I was feeling stronger than I had ever felt as a man—as a person. I was thinking about each painful part of my life and how it was all a necessary part of the process. Growth through struggle was making me strong enough to be able to climb to the next level. Whatever life dished out at me, I would be equipped with the right tools to handle it.

I was doing it!

Paul always said, "Whatever doesn't kill you makes you stronger." He had a trunk full of those trite feel-better-about-yourself expressions.

"Time heals all wounds," a personal favorite of mine and one that currently had me on the ropes. "Time heals all wounds" was becoming a reality that made me sad and scared all at the same time. I didn't want time to heal all wounds—my wounds. I held the pain close to my heart because I felt that once the pain was gone, the relationship would be gone as well. It would be over with Laura, and we would be out of each other's lives forever.

Ughhhhhhhhhh! Enough already!

We had just hit a brief pocket of turbulence, which smacked me with the realization that Jane and I had become much closer than we were before I got to Tempe. It was a teary farewell for both of us. When I said good-bye to Jane, she went on and on about the stories I told everyone about my journey, perspective, and attitude—she said I put ideas into their friends' heads to contemplate. I wasn't really sure what Jane was talking about. I don't remember telling anyone anything of major substance or importance to contemplate.

Saying good-bye to Jane was just as sentimental and weird as had been our "hello" when I arrived at their doorstep. Jane hugged me even more tightly when I left . The last thing she said was, "Thanks, Johnny Appleseed. We won't forget you!" I can still picture her waving good-bye from the balcony.

At that point, I was so done with the plane ride. I wished that I was already home. The wait was painful—sheer torture! I was suffering the anticipation of a child waiting to open presents the day before Christmas. "Will I be getting what I want or just opening a bunch of pretty boxes of things other people wanted me to have."

In another hour, I would be off the plane. I hated the red eye! Relax, Mr. Cool. Soon enough, I would be home and having a beer with The Boys. I could taste it all.

Part IV

Home

Chapter 16

Home

I couldn't believe that I had been home for over a week. For all intents and purposes, I should have already been back in the desert. The time back home was more than I could have ever anticipated.

Just as expected, when I landed, The Boys were there to pick me up and kept me out all day. It was 6:30 a.m. when the plane landed. The minutes went roughly like this:

I got off the plane, and The Boys were there waiting for me with beer in hand. We decided to go down memory lane and visit the old haunts. First, we went to the diner; and the waitress didn't want to serve us drinks at such an early hour. Money talks, she brought us each a beer—probably more like four beers. We went to the trestle, a place where we would meet before the high school bell rang during senior year to drink beer—had a couple of more beers in remembrance. For crappy hour, we ended up at the Scrounge Lounge, which was the local dive strip joint. We sat like little boys in our usual spot in the corner, far enough away from the action, but close enough to get a peek at girls who shouldn't be taking their clothes off in the first place. Anyone who has been to the Lounge knows what I'm talking about. At the Lounge, we never talked to anyone or did anything, it was just a taboo place where the drinks had an entertainment charge built in. We laughed all day until it hurt. I had to get home.

My parents were noticeably disappointed at the timing of my arrival through their front door and into their loving arms. The fact that I wasn't as sober as they would have liked didn't help matters.

Fortunately, the disappointment only lasted until we hugged each other; they were just glad I was home.

The funny thing about family is that for some odd reason you are more apt to let them down than your friends because they are your family. It's odd—there is a strong tendency to take your family's feelings for granted. Of course, they will understand because they basically have no choice, after all, they will always be your family. On the other side of things, you choose your friends, and they can choose not to be your friends. It seems that because there is a choice, the people you love the most are the ones who pay the penalty. I guess when you look at it that way; your family probably doesn't see the funny thing about "family."

Home was home, although everything seemed smaller, my parents seemed older, the refrigerator seemed fuller. The first thing I did was to go into every room, and then I looked through the refrigerator and took an inventory. Finally, the long overnight plane ride, the general excitement of being home, and probably the boozing with The Boys since 6:30 a.m. took its toll and I crashed hard on the couch in front of a cozy fire.

While I was home, I visited with as many people as possible. All the people who cared about me wanted a piece of me—there just wasn't enough of me to go around. I kept hearing my mother tell everyone, "We never see him, he's hardly home at all, he's burning the candle at both ends and in the middle!"

I did feel special and loved, but the one person who could have really made a difference was Laura—and she didn't even call. My last letter to her did say when I was coming home. Laura knew I was back; she could call.

It was a mandatory tradition to visit my godfather who also happened to be my cool Uncle Charlie. We partied together to celebrate my departure, and it only made sense to party with him while I was back. We cooked up a feast, drank many bottles of wine, and laughed at ridiculous family nonsense.

To cap the night off, because it was part of the tradition, we smoked cigars and drank cognac like gentlemen, with our feet up

Home

in front of a blazing fire. My Uncle Charlie passed out, which was also a tradition, and I talked to his wife, Camilla, until I passed out. "Nothing exceeds like excess" is the motto at my uncle's house. That was the home I missed.

While I was home, it was imperative that I go bowling with my brothers, Joe and John, and my sister-in-law, Gabrielle. My brothers and I were always very competitive regardless of the sport, task, or social situation. It had always been a kill-or-be-killed environment in everything we did. Remember, nothing is sweeter than being able to say, "I told you so," or "I won," or "You lost."

My brothers and I are very different individuals; we act and react differently to the same situations. The perfect example was when I originally left home and Joe cried and John couldn't be bothered.

We started, as we always did, by going to the Chinese restaurant next door to the bowling alley while we waited for our lanes. After all we needed the proper bowling primer—two famous, big-bucket, umbrella-decorated, Super Scorpion bowls with a flaming floater of 151 rum and 4 straws along with a couple of pu pu platters.

When we bowled, it was our tradition to take on pseudo bowling nicknames and to refer to each other by them. Mel, Trixie, Alice, Flo, Jughead, Ralph, Norton are all good bowling names. Somehow, it never remained nice and friendly for long.

Juggs Verylarge—is a classic name for Gabby, and a good example of what I'm talking about.

Watching Gabby bowl was always a hoot. She had this three-steps-forward, two-steps-back approach, until she finally got to the foul line, stopped dead, brought her arm back, and let it go. Gabby getting drunk on whiskey sours was also pretty funny to watch—it only took one and a half drinks to get the show to start.

You know things are getting out of hand when someone pages Gabby over the PA system as "Pussy Galore! Will Pussy Galore, please report to lane 29? It's your turn to bowl."

We drank and we bowled. Once again, I was Kingpin, I was better than they were, I won; they lost and I told them so—as usual.

My story—enough said.

That was the home that I missed.

Chapter 17

The Wedding

The reason I was back in the first place—the wedding of the century—made returning home even more meaningful. Richard and Silvia were high school sweethearts finally realizing their life-long dreams—this time sharing it with others. I can still remember them trying to sneak away off campus back in high school as if they were so clever. They thought they were fooling the school administrators, and they also thought they were fooling their friends. One time, The Boys tied a string of cans to the back of Richard's car along with a "just married" sign. Without a clue, he and Silvia fooled no one, as they skipped class for a little afternoon delight to the sound of the clanking cans trailing behind them.

Richard and Silvia made me feel important, and I was immensely touched by the way they included me in their wedding plans. They started by inviting me to the rehearsal dinner, which was a very nice family affair held at the Travelers Rest—one of the nicer restaurants in Westchester. Additionally, Richard and Silvia had me, along with Paul and Jack, sit with them at the bride and groom's dais at the reception, which really moved me.

The reception was held at the Tarrytown House, a beautiful historic mansion overlooking the scenic Hudson River. It was converted into a hotel to cater weddings and special events. Because the Tarrytown House was a mansion first, and not originally designed to be a hotel or conference center, it had a comforting charm. Even though the wedding party was spread over two floors, we were still in close proximity because the tables located on the balcony wrapped around the room. There were several adjoining rooms off of the balcony with wide and very tall open doorways that welcomed all the guests to the party. The dance floor was right in the middle of the first floor and, like a stadium with the stage in the center, the action was right there no matter where you were. So the dynamic layout of the mansion created a vertical party as well as horizontal. It was like having a wedding at someone's really nice home versus a catering hall or country club—very cool idea.

With one hand nervously adjusting his tie and the other nonchalantly holding his bottle of beer, Paul pulled off the best man speech to end all best man speeches. He pulled the speech out of his ass—the speech was classic; Paul was classic! Albeit, the moment was broken when he had to share the spotlight with Silvia's lesbian sister's maid-of-honor speech. I know, what the hell is a maid-of-honor speech? It was a new and different concept to us—not so much the lesbian part, but the speech part. Equal time for women, I guess.

After the reception, we continued the party down below the Biddle Mansion in the Sleepy Hollow Pub, which by itself was very cool, but to accentuate the ambiance, there is one of the first, fully automated bowling lanes ever built in the middle of this authentic dimly lit pub. The party raged on for hours! We drank, we danced, and we were merry.

As the night came to a close, as I remember it, we weren't wearing pants when we left the pub—always the sign of a good party.

The first of two glorious shinning moments to be remembered, gossiped about at parties, and most importantly—something to be proud of—happened near the end of the night. I had the distinguished honor of helping Silvia, the newly wedded bride; throw up in the ladies room. What a scene: Silvia, the beautiful bride still dressed in her wedding day whites, was on her knees, with one hand on the toilet for support and the other hand in her mouth inducing herself to relieve the nausea she was experiencing. There I was holding her hair out of the way of the splattering vomit

The Wedding

and rubbing her back trying to make it all better—another sign of a good party. Meanwhile, the entire time, I was looking for my camera and, of course, The Boys!

I couldn't wait to tell The Boys, so we could bust Richard's balls. Remember, any chance you get—it's always Friends Fuck Friends—Over. FFFO was The Boys' motto. And, when it comes to The Boys, it's better to fuck than be fucked—believe me; I had been on both sides of FFFO. Given enough time, everybody eventually takes a turn bending over. Just like in Vegas, if you keep playing, the odds are you're gonna catch a beating. And in life let's face it, every once in a while, everybody gets a beating.

On your hands and knees making love to a toilet bowl on the night you should be making love to your husband is one way to start off married life. Ironically, Silvia read Richard the riot act before the wedding, warning him not to do what turns out she had done. Do as I say not as I do, I guess. I wonder if it was a sign from God. This was the kind of sign that could have *triple goocher* potential. As always, time will tell.

I'm sure it'll work out. FFFO.

Shinning Moment Number Two came when tough guy Jack had us traveling to a nearby bar after the wedding was over. Jack felt we hadn't had enough alcohol after a full day of drinking, but it was more likely because we were going home empty handed and he felt we needed to keep hope alive by changing venues. Of course, that was until he had me grab the wheel so he could puke out of the moving car's driver-side window. With that glory, the wedding of the century and the evening came to a close.

As much as I loved being home, I decided that I could never come back to stay—although deep down it will always be my home. It was comforting to know that I could always go back if I had to, but it was the same comfort zone that would keep me from ever going back to that home I left behind.

It was great being home, but in the back of my mind, there was an itch that I tried not to scratch. I waited until the last couple of days before I called Laura. When I first got home, I wanted to call Laura because my time was short and I was only supposed to be back for a long weekend. Once it had been a week past my scheduled return, I realized that Laura wasn't going to call me. Just as I kept putting off taking my road trip, I put off calling Laura. I've always been one of the great procrastinators of all time.

I wasn't going to let Laura ruin my visit home. I figured that if Laura rejected me, only the last day would suck like a wet rag on a cold day, and I would be happy to be return to the Life and Times of Nick Anthony—On the Road. I had to keep perspective; the facts were the facts. I hadn't been in contact with Laura for months.

I felt that as long as I didn't call her, she couldn't say "no" to seeing me. I was keeping hope alive by not calling her. It was a constant battle, because on one hand, I did want to see her so badly, on the other hand, I wanted Laura to call me on her own.

Chapter 18

The Call

Enough was enough! The time finally came for me to go back on the road—I couldn't postpone my return any longer. It was time to pick up the dice and let them roll. It was time to call Laura.

Of course, I had an "If she says this, then I will say that," game plan. I painstakingly tried to work out every possible detail in every possible scenario. Before I rolled for the big money, I ran the game plan by my two confidants, Gabby and Paul.

The game plan was simply as follows:
1. I wasn't going to get tied up in small talk or in a conversation about what was new in our lives. If she would see me, we could talk about it then, and if she wouldn't see me, it didn't really matter anyway.
2. I would take charge and just tell her that I wanted to see her; I would see her and that was that. Take no prisoners!
3. Wear the sandals. They couldn't hurt.

That was the whole plan in a nutshell.

Life comes down to a few moments, and this is another one of them.

The idea was to call Laura at work to increase the chances of reaching her. I picked up the phone, dialed it, and, as the phone rang, my anxiety, which was at a feverish pitch, disappeared. I was, however, pacing up a storm.

Laura answered the phone and sounded glad to hear from me.

"I'm glad you called," she said. "I've been thinking about you, and I was going to call you."

"Really??!?!" I said.

Laura knew I was coming home for the wedding, and I was only going to be in town for the weekend. When was she going to call me? I should already be back on the road.

At the word go, Laura was into a full-blown, excitement-driven conversation.

"I have so many things to tell you!" she started. "So many revelations! I want to hear about your trip! Every detail! I'm so glad you called!"

I was concentrating on my game plan, and I was so nervous, that everything Laura said became so blurry I couldn't process what she was saying. I was just looking for a break, an opening—any opportunity.

Finally, it looked good. Here goes...

"Listen, Laura," I said, jumping in, "we can talk on the phone, but I'm only going to be home for the next three days, and I want to see you before I leave."

Now, the dice were out of my mouth, rolling down the table, bouncing off the back bumper. I was prepared for snake eyes.

"I can't, this isn't a good time for me right now," she said.

Snake eyes—perfect! At that moment, my heart stopped, and my head felt like it exploded all over the room. I listened for the deathblow plunger of ridiculous excuses that filled my veins with paralyzing venom and that had become so annoying.

"Tonight is all wrong," she said. "I have to work until 5 p.m. tomorrow, and I ... how about ... is it okay if we meet after 5 p.m. tomorrow night? Where do you want to meet?"

What just happened? Did I understand her correctly; is this a reprieve? I frantically tried piecing my head back together as fast as I could. I couldn't believe it; Laura said "yes." I wasn't prepared with the "where" because that was the one scenario that slipped through the cracks in preparing my conversation game plan.

The Call

We decided to haunt Oliver's Bar and Restaurant—one of our many old hangouts.

Fucking psychdog! I was pumped! "Yes!" What a wonderful word.

Maybe I was reading this the wrong way. Maybe this would be Laura's way of ending things completely—a new clean break without any loose ends. After all, what was the reason she initially said, "This isn't a good time?" Was it because she had a new boyfriend? The new boyfriend would be there for sure. Whatever the reason for her seeing me, it couldn't be good. I hadn't heard from her in weeks, no beeps, no birthday anything, no nothing.

I wasn't two minutes into my victory dance when a whole new wave of worries came crashing down on my head. Wipe out! It's back—the manifestation of my old self couldn't be uglier!

No, no, no, fuck all this noise! Get it back together! That was the old Nick, I convinced myself. The new me: *I don't care if she comes, stays, lays, or prays: whatever happens, my toes are still tappin'.*

I called Paul to tell him I wouldn't be joining him and Jack tomorrow night, and he said, "What the fuck—you're not meeting us out?!"

"I have a date," I said.

"You bagged the elephant, wow!" Paul said. "Whatever you do, don't tell Jack you called Laura, he'll go ballistic! He finally thinks you're moving on and forgetting about her, and will try to prevent it."

Wasn't the situation stressful enough without the pressure from Jack?

I pleaded with Paul. "Listen, you can't tell Jack, not yet, he'll try talking me out of it, and I don't feel like being a phony right now."

One of the many hard parts of this situation was that I couldn't confide in many of the closest people in my life about what was going on in my head. They just couldn't or wouldn't understand. They thought they were helping me out by telling me to move on and forget about Laura. They would say I should date other people and stop calling and so on. It didn't help!

I knew they cared and that they had my best interests at heart, but I just didn't want to hear it. Sooooo—I didn't put myself in the position. I'm not saying that it stopped or prevented people from preaching to me—it just cut down on the number of times I had to deal with it.

From the beginning, I wasn't ready to quit, not like that anyway. Under the circumstances, I hoped to have the courage to never quit. Quitting is so easy.

The two people who I could really talk to about the Laura situation were Paul and Gabby. They listened, somehow understood my feelings, and kept me in check.

Paul was happy for me. When I told him about my revived doubts, he said, "Forget about it! She can smell it on you, it's 1994, this is your year, things are changing, going your way, you're a traveler, you've been to the desert, for Christ sake, snap out of it!"

When I told Paul I was thinking about wearing the sandals, he said, "Now that's crazy! It's as out-of-bounds as a bride puking her guts up because she drank too much at her own wedding."

Before I got off the phone with Paul, he said, "Tell her new boyfriend I said hello."

Like I've said: Friends Fuck Friends Over!

"Nice talk," I said to Paul. "I'll tell him. Listen, I have to go. Tomorrow I'll either be out late or I'll be back by 9 p.m., and I'll hook up with you and Jack."

"Cool, good luck," Paul said.

"Thanks, I'll need it."

Now, it was Gabby's turn. Gabrielle wasn't only my brother's wife, my chief confidant, and psychotherapist, but a very good friend. Gabby was the only person who knew my inner thoughts on most things. Gabby was a great listener with the bedside manner of a Catholic nurse. I had told her everything, and at that point, I could tell her anything. I told her about some of my concerns, and she told me not to worry. "Things will go fine," she said.

The Call

"Why was Laura going to see me now?" I asked Gabby. "I haven't seen her since right before Thanksgiving. She wouldn't even see me before I left. Why now?"

Gabby tried to reassure me that not that much time had gone by and that I shouldn't worry about the reasons why Laura hadn't agreed to see me until now.

"I know," I said. "I'm just expecting the worst and hoping for a nice night out with her. In reality, there isn't anything more she can ask for back—she has everything already, she has The Key."

"Well, that's a good and healthy way to approach the situation," Gabby said. "You shouldn't plan for the worst or get your hopes up to high, either."

"If Laura refused to see me, I wouldn't even be concerned right now," I said. "Don't get me wrong, I'd be pissed off, which would help me deal with the whole situation."

"You sound fine," Gabby said. "Keep remembering how far you've come and everything that you've been through. Call me as soon as you get back tomorrow night!"

Chapter 19

My Mother

The night before my date with Laura, my mother brought home Chinese takeout for dinner. There are few of life's delights that are more enjoyable than good Chinese takeout and ice-cold beer at your own kitchen table. It reminded me of high school days. Eating takeout at home when I didn't feel like being with the rest of the world was always very comforting. I didn't really feel like being social at that point. My Work Smirk was just getting primed for the twenty-four-hour wait.

Having my parents together at the table, I thought it might be a good time to have a discussion about some of my reflections. I finally had the proof that might help me change my mothers' way of thinking. The evidence I had was concrete and irrefutable and she would have to admit she was wrong and tell me that I made a good decision when I bought my car.

I interrogated my mother. "Do you remember what you said to me when I brought my first brand new car home?" I asked her.

Recalling almost exactly she said, "It was cute but too small in the back for passengers, and two doors made it hard to load and unload groceries."

"Yes, you did say that but, you also said that I couldn't move a couch with the car if I had to," I said. "I've had the car for so many years and it's still the single best purchase of my life. I paid it off and have had no car payments for years—truly a bonus. Besides the occasional tires and brakes, I've never had to do a thing except to change the oil. It has 130,000 miles on the original clutch, and has now traveled across the country stuffed to the gills with my bare necessities. It has gone from the Empire State, through the Smoky Mountains, to both ends of the Grand Canyon, almost to heaven at Mesa Verde in Colorado, though Utah—Bryce, Zion, The Arches..." I caught my breath to continue. "In all of this time, across all of those miles, I've never had to move one couch—not once!"

"Yes," she said, "but the point is, you couldn't move one if you did have to."

"Who can argue with your thinking? You're amazingly consistent. And, you're right, it was obviously a huge mistake to buy this car."

I was beaten and finally gave up.

I've always been open with my parents, which has made for a special relationship. I'm outspoken and say what I believe. Sometimes they don't always like what I have to say, but I'm honest and speak from my heart. I have a very dry, sarcastic sense of humor, which takes time for some people to figure out. At times, I think, my parents still have problems with it. I think the truth scares people, and when I come at them, they may be faced with some truths that they might not like to deal with.

While we sat at the table, I told my mother and father the latest developments on the Laura front. Of course, they seemed glad for me, but I could tell they tried to hide their concern. They knew how much damage I had endured and were concerned about me having a relapse and completely losing it.

Couldn't they see how much I'd grown from this whole experience? How much stronger I'd become? Even still, my parents had been supportive and understanding since the beginning of this mess. I didn't know how they knew, but at times they understood better than I did. I figured the experiences of their lives guided them.

I gave my parents a lot of credit; they knew that I had been through a lot and they showed me some faith. Of course, my mother wouldn't be my mother without riddling me with fear

My Mother

about something I already knew—that I shouldn't expect too much and that I should be careful.

I knew to be cautious. Without risks, there were no rewards. Why couldn't my mother see that?

Be safe, have a good job, have security, make money, don't take risks. My great grandmother drilled those values into my grandmother's head, and my grandmother drilled that into my mother's head, and my mother had been drilling it into my head. When will it end?

After dinner, my mother asked, "Does anyone want any espresso?"

I had to laugh. This keeps everybody frozen at the table, which keeps the family together a little bit longer, which, in return makes my mother happy.

I need to stop trying to get my mother to be somebody she's not. She is who she is which is a big reason why I am who I am. And, I am very fortunate and thankful.

While the espresso was brewing, I broke out the newspaper and read the horoscopes—not that I put much stock in them—of course.

For Aquarius, my sign, under "Tendencies for Tomorrow" it read, "An anticipated meeting will go much better than expected."

Are you fucking kidding me?! Are the gods actually watching, putting everyone else on earth aside this day and allowing me to see what they're planning?

I had to admit that I was more than intrigued. Maybe it was my year, maybe it was the sandals, or the attitude, or maybe it was the beers with dinner and Sambuca with the coffee. I didn't care what it was; it sounded positive. I was keeping things in perspective and looking ahead for any low-hanging branches.

Chapter 20

Game Day

Everything else was a prelude to this—this date. This opportunity with Laura was what I wanted, wasn't it? Game day was upon me, and I'm sure I was a real bear to be around.

The hours before the date were uncomfortable to say the least. I went from room to room with the good old reliable Work Smirk on, opening cabinets and closing cabinets, opening the door to the refrigerator and closing the door to the refrigerator. There wasn't anything in any of those places; I just felt the need to check them every two minutes. I wasn't very sociable. I was just satisfied to be in the comfort of my parent's home.

The primping was complete and then it was time to go.

A car with smoked windows was parked exactly perpendicular to my car—apparently blocking my forward progress.

"Who the hell's car is out there blocking my car?" I said under my breath. It was probably no big deal. I would just back up and go around it. *Why would someone park like that? Oh shit, it's fucking J a c k.* That made sense. *Shit!* I really didn't feel like dealing with this.

"Jackkkkkk, what's going on?" I asked.

"Nothin', I'm here to pick your ass up. We're goin' out tonight," he said. "What, did you forget?" he added, clearly pretending not to know anything.

"Obviously, you talked to Paul," I said.

"Yeah, that's right, tough guy," he said. "I hear you're blowin' us off, and I have a few things to say about dat." He had to get out of his car to impart his words of wisdom.

"All right, let's hear it," I said, preparing to "yes" him to death.

"What the fuck are you wearing on your feet?!"

He laughed then quickly returned to Jack Johnson, Marlboro Man. I still couldn't believe that the government gave him a gun and a badge. Sometimes I really thought he bought into all that shit. Sometimes I thought the government didn't know what the hell they were doing.

Jack's machismo (I hate the word "machismo" but that described it perfectly) melted and he stammered, "I just wanted you to—ah. To—ah. To, ah, tell Laura I said, 'hello.' I wish I had the guts to stick things out like you have. I really hope things work out. But be careful, watch yourself, my brother!"

"Thanks, man. I appreciate it. You're a good friend."

"The best," he said.

We hugged and, while Jack saddled up, he laughingly asked, "Was Silvia really on her hands and knees with her head in the toilet? Did you take any pictures?"

If Jack would have left without telling me to be careful I would have thought it was a bad sign. He pulled away with his G–Ride—lights flashing and half of his tires left on the pavement in front of my parent's house.

He always left something behind.

Part V

The Date

Chapter 21

The Wait

The drive down to Oliver's was torturous. I wore a pair of Dockers, a nice shirt, and obviously, the sandals. I was looking and feeling fine. I had the aloofness of the artist and the coolness of a confident man—with my buds watching my back. What more could a man ask for?

A daring man takes what he wants—I told myself.

All day long, I had been questioning everything. It was draining after a while. I finally got to the point where I couldn't take questioning myself anymore. It was time to be a warrior. I shifted into low gear, saving myself for the battle ahead. It helped telling myself that Laura was probably walking around with her own Work Smirk on and was nervous about seeing me.

I parked in the usual spot in the underground garage and didn't notice Laura's car in the lot. That just gave me more time to wait and wonder. I sat in the "God spot" at the bar—so I could see everyone in the place, as well as everyone coming in or going out of both entrances.

As cool as I tried to be, I was nervous as hell, and my eyes kept drying out because I was wearing my contacts. I kept changing my position like a lunatic. I'm sure anyone watching me was having themselves a good laugh.

I put my hands on the bar; I took my hands off the bar. I put my hands in my pocket; I took my hands out of my pocket. I put my feet on the rail; I took my feet off the rail. Should I be sitting or should I be standing? You know, all the things that will would probably make all the difference in the world when Laura walked in with her new boyfriend. I could hear him say to her, "Can you believe that guy had his hands on the bar? What an asshole!"

Finally it hit me. I came to the realization that I was in a bar where they just happened to have the cure for nerves. The medicine I took first was Guinness. They certainly didn't have the selection that they had on the road, but you can never go wrong with a Guinness.

The questioning continued. Do I kiss her hello? If I do kiss her, do I kiss her on the lips or cheek or do I just hug her? *Fuck all these stupid-ass questions!*

I was ready for my next dose of medicine and there was no sign of Laura. I didn't want to get drunk before she got there—how ludicrous would that be? Maybe she decided not to come after all.

If Laura didn't show up, I would have to make up some story that she did, because I couldn't go back and tell everyone that she was a no-show. If that happened, I would have no choice but to submit and let her go.

I ordered another beer and decided to play some music on the juke.

My list:

"Brown-Eyed Girl"—Van Morrison—Laura is my brown-eyed girl.

"Wonderful Tonight"—Eric Clapton—my all-time favorite.

"Come Monday"—Jimmy Buffett—master-relaxer.

"Piano Man"—Billy Joel—We all have a dream.

I wondered if I was in this situation because I never asked Laura to marry me. After all, we were both married to other people in a previous life before we got together. Getting married again never seemed to matter much to either of us, I figured. I mean we never talked about it. Maybe marriage mattered to her, and I just didn't know it. I just wish I could have one more chance to ask her to marry me. Maybe I would ask Laura to marry me—tonight. *Please! That would look so desperate. Ask Laura to marry me? Are you listening to yourself? Tonight she's going to tell you good-bye once and*

The Wait

for all. I couldn't stand the idea of seeing her with someone else laughing or being intimate; I couldn't get it out of my head.

I wondered what Laura would be wearing and how she would look. Would her hair be short or long, curly or straight? Maybe she wouldn't even look the same; maybe she would look like someone else.

I wondered so often what Laura was going through. There wasn't a day that went by that I didn't wonder about that. Unfortunately, I only had my imagination to tell me what was going on. Laura never let me in.

I felt as though I was the one variable, the only variable that Laura pushed out of her life. Laura used to say that she had the tendency to hurt the people closest to her—she was so right in this case.

There were so many things that I didn't know, after all, Laura, was only 28. I did try to understand and make sense of it all. I read as much as I could, but reading only gets you so far.

Maybe I was judging my past too harshly. I was such a fool.

Maybe the sandals were all wrong. *No, she'll get a kick out of 'em.* Just the fact that I felt comfortable enough to wear sandals showed a certain amount of confidence. I had that whole artist thing going on. Forget about the sandals being all wrong. They were all right!

I needed a freakin' team of psychiatrists concentrating solely on me, around the clock!

I got up to check the jukebox again, and this time when I turned around to go back to my seat, there she was standing in front of me. Laura completely caught me off guard. All my fidgeting, all my trying to control every aspect of the evening was for nothing.

When I finally saw Laura, she had already seen me and was smiling from ear to ear. Her smile was contagious, and she was just as beautiful as I had remembered. And I'm not talking about pretty; I'm talking about stunning, gorgeous. Webster's definition of gorgeous: "splendidly brilliant, showy, magnificent."

We walked closer to each other, paused for a minute to look in each other's eyes, kissed on the lips, and tightly embraced each other. When it came down to it, all the planning in the world was out the window.

Laura was wearing a turquoise outfit with one of her trademark scarves and looked fantastic.

She told me I looked great and said, looking down at my feet, "Birkenstocks!"

"Hey, I've been to the desert!" I said. "You look fantastic! What would you like to drink?"

"Whatever you're drinking," she said.

I ordered two more beers.

With all of her enthusiasm, Laura ran on like a freight train as she spoke, it was hard not to smile and feel good.

"I have all these things to tell you," she began, "these new revelations, things my therapist has brought out and other things that I've realized on my own."

I loved her enthusiasm. It was pure electricity. I wasn't sure where this was all going, but I couldn't take my eyes and ears off her. I was smiling so hard it hurt, and that had to be good. I wasn't sure if I was about to have my legs chopped out from under me, but at that moment, just to watch her so happy was enough for me not to care.

"I'm done with the chemo and I start radiation treatments soon," she went on. "It's amazing how much better I feel without that poison circulating through my body. It will be some time before it is completely out of my system, but it's as though a cloud has been lifted. I wanted to just come here casual with a baseball cap on but I didn't want to get changed at work."

I was surprised she made that comment. It was as if she were saying she would feel comfortable enough with me to just wear a baseball cap. I guessed that also meant that her hair hadn't grown back yet.

"I told my therapist that you were everything I wanted in a man to marry, except I didn't feel as though you were ambitious enough," she said. "You are the most romantic, most sensitive, considerate man in the world. Through the therapy, I discovered that you left the safety of home to check out the world, become a photographer, and do what we both needed.

How more ambitious could you be? You are doing it!"

Laura said it all!

Then she talked about her parents and why she has this issue with ambition. I think she was nervous and just as glad to see me as I was to see her.

Laura told me that after radiation she was planning to move to Boston—a place that we were supposed to move together, before she was diagnosed with breast cancer. She wanted to know what I thought. I felt uneasy about the question because I saw an opportunity to expose myself to pain. I needed to make a power play. Now was the time to take my shot!

"Well," I said, "that all depends, are you talking about moving to Boston with me or without me?"

Had I really just put my head out on the chopping block?

Laura responded cautiously as if she were worried about what my reaction to her response would be, and then she said, cautiously, "With you?"

I smiled and said, "Yes, I would definitely consider that."

Laura looked happy and relieved all at the same time. I couldn't believe how well things were going.

I told her about my goal to live in different places in the country at different times of the year. There were so many great cities and towns in this country; they should all be enjoyed at their best times.

She looked at me with excitement when I talked. Her lips would move when I spoke as if she were excited about every word that I had to say; it was something that I missed about her this whole time that I was away.

Finally, we started talking, really communicating, about the issues that led up to our split up—some issues I learned along my journey and some other things that Laura enlightened me about that I just couldn't have imagined. The lights at the bar dimmed a bit and then appeared to be brighter than they were.

I told Laura about a woman I met during my travels who had explained some of the psychological torture a person goes through when they're dealing with a serious health issue—certain *guilts*.

"It used to bother me when you would tell me that maybe I wouldn't lose my hair, and you seemed to put so much emphasis on me losing my hair," Laura said. "I just couldn't deal with the way I thought you felt when my hair started falling out. Remember the time you rubbed my neck in the parking lot? I was so worried you were going to knock off my wig that I almost lost my mind."

I couldn't believe it, it was the complete opposite in my mind.

"I thought losing your hair meant so much to you that I was trying to let you know it didn't mean anything to me," I told her. "It didn't matter one bit to me if you lost your hair."

That was a perfect example of the miscommunication and unknowing guilt that the woman I had met on the road was talking about. Laura was worried about me rejecting her. I had no idea. So much more was making sense. I realized then that our issues had begun when her hair started falling out.

There were *guilts* a person just couldn't realize, such as if I said, "Oh, you look good today," Laura might think what if he doesn't say that today or the next, maybe I don't look good today, maybe I'm dying, oh my God!"

Or if I said, "I love you, you mean everything to me." That put on a lot of pressure because Laura might see herself as having to live and be there for me and if she died, what would I do. She would want to protect me, so she would push me away.

Laura told me that she thought that I would make a great father some day, and she didn't want to take that away from me because she probably shouldn't have children. I told her that we could always adopt and be able to bring up children the way we want. That was something I thought about when I was on the road. I never would have considered that when I was younger. I always thought that I had to have my own children or no children. Life was funny that way.

Laura was thinking and agonizing about all these things at age 28. It wasn't fair. It made me sick; it made me angry!

All along, I had stood by the concept that love conquered all things, great and small. I basically refused to respect the power that any illness could have or hold on the past, present, and future. That was my biggest miscalculation. I had been a fool.

It was as if we both understood each other for the first time in over eight months. It seemed as *if awakening from denial was a slow but necessary process.* We were both communicating, and it was making sense, finally.

I told Laura that I spoke with her friend Mina, who gave me great advice that saved my sanity a couple of times. Of course, there were times that nothing would help because I couldn't remember where I had put my mind.

Mina told me not to take it personally if Laura didn't want to talk with me on the phone, that she was going through hell with all of the treatments. Not knowing what Laura was going through killed me. That lack of control was something that frustrated me the most. I wanted to be there for her.

"Mina said that sometimes you didn't want to talk to anyone, not her, not your family, no one," I told Laura. "I did take it personally, how could I not? I felt like I was the only one shut out of your life. That was when I started writing letters instead of calling you. If you weren't in the mood, you could read them when you were."

"I loved your letters," Laura said. "I love the way you write, it's like the way you talk. Your letters helped me feel as though I were with you all the time. I could pick them up anytime and relive the time with you."

Bang!

I was still feeling a bit standoffish; I didn't want to jump in with both feet, not yet. Well, I did want to jump in with both feet, but in my mind, Jack and my mother were sitting right there having drinks with us. I just wasn't sure where all this was going, but Laura was saying everything I wanted to hear, everything.

On the drive down to meet Laura, I was trying to figure out how to save face with The Boys when I was able to meet them out by 9 p.m. How wrong I was? Again.

Laura told me about the possibility of going to Italy after all her treatments were over.

"There is no one I would like to share Italy with more than you, but I'm not sure if I should do this by myself," she said.

I could understand that.

At this point, I was just hoping that the possibility of getting back together was real. There was so much I could understand, now.

While we were in the bar holding hands across the table, staring into each other's eyes, laughing and reminiscing, I wanted to absorb her into myself. I wanted to make love to her, I wanted to cuddle, I wanted to wrap her up into me and never let her go.

I didn't believe my wants were possible, I didn't know what was going on in her head. Other things were now at work in my head.

She had some revelations, she needed to talk to me, she wanted to call but didn't.

Everything she said so far was positive—when was she going to lower the boom as she has done so many times in the past?

Laura told me that her friend Liz was so happy that we were going to see each other and that she said to say "hello." That meant a lot to me because, in the beginning, Laura told me that her friends and family thought it was fine that we broke up. I was hurt to think that the people on her side of things didn't care whether we were together, and it reassured me that they did.

From Oliver's, we decided to go to a place just down the street for dinner. It wasn't far; we could walk. It was drizzling, and there was a nip in the air. I wanted to put my arm around her, but I was cautious about getting too familiar too fast. So, I just started

The Wait

walking alongside her. Laura grabbed my arm, and we walked arm and arm, smiling in the light mist.

This all seemed to be a dream, I couldn't believe one thing that was happening. *Please don't let me wake up, not yet.* Then out of nowhere, she said smiling, "I just want you to know that I'm not going to sleep with you tonight."

Who-ha!

And just like that, an impossible thought became a real possibility. That meant she was thinking about it and that I had to find away to make it happen.

I just kept smiling and said, "OooooKay."

While we were walking, Laura told me that her friend had asked her before she left work, "So are you going to get any tonight or what?" Laura told me that her sister asked her the same question. I thought this was very interesting because it backed up my new assumptions.

This new information gave me even more confidence about everything. Laura was looking forward to this date, she told everyone about it and they were glad, too. She must have told them about this date in a positive way because they were asking questions that they wouldn't be asking if this was the big blow-off good-bye.

We both giggled while we walked in the rain, looking at each other and then looking ahead, laughing like school kids on a first date. We were laughing because we were both nervous and because neither one of us could believe any of these thoughts were running through our minds, let alone coming out of our mouths.

Then Laura asked me whether I had been intimate with anyone else since her. "No," I said. "But not that I didn't try, of course." She laughed. Then, I asked her the same question and she said, "No, of course, not." Suddenly, I felt that was a stupid question to ask.

We each ordered a glass of merlot at the bar of a trendy Italian restaurant in White Plains, while we waited for them to set up our table. Laura needed to freshen up in the ladies room, and I went to our table to contemplate the evening up to that point. I could hear

Paul saying, "It's 1994, it's your year, things are going your way, she can smell the desert on you."

We had been to this restaurant before, but everything seemed different this time. The whole night, everything seemed different—better. My prayers were certainly being answered, but it was all going too well. I needed to be cautious.

I had to come up with a plan to get back to her place and make love with the love of my life. Laura was giving me a fucking hall pass, for Pete's sake. Now I'm saying "for Pete's sake" again. The pictures: I still had to find a way to show her some pictures from the road—that just might be the ticket!

Then, it came time to order—a part of dining out that I've always hated. I hate ordering because a person shouldn't have to make decisions when there are so many wonderful delights from which to choose.

Laura was more than happy to decide for both of us, and then we could split everything. She smiled with excitement. It was a joy to watch her order because she was so enthusiastic about it. She tapped on her bottom lip with her index finger as she tried to decide the perfect combination of food and wine.

Sharing with Laura was truly enjoyable. For the first time in a long time, food and wine had taste. I wasn't sure if it ever would again, and somehow it was better than I remembered.

After dinner and a bottle of wine, she asked in her sexy luscious voice, "Should we have a cup-a-chino, Guy?" I never did say no. "Guy" was an endearing nickname we interchangeably referred to each other by.

I started getting anxious about dinner winding down and the night ending. We continued to hold hands and smile at each other across the table like we both knew a valuable secret.

Still looking for my opportunity, the check now on the table, I saw my next shot and took it.

"I want you to see the pictures I took."

"Yes, definitely." she said. "Yes, but where? I can't wait!"

The Wait

And then, without further provocation from me, she tilted her head down and looked up at me with those beautiful, brown bedroom eyes and said, "Well, we could go back to my place."

Yes! There it was! Yes, yes, yes! I tried to be cool, but it was close to impossible. Like when I drove my '69 Buick Electra 225 convertible down the street with the top down and music from *Miami Vice* blasting out of the speakers—I couldn't help but smile. Of course, that was before my ex-wife took the car and sold it for one dollar, because as she said, "All you love is this car!" Fuck! That's a whole other story...

"Oooo-Kay by me, if it's OooKay with you," I said. While looking at the brass ring.

"Remember what I told you earlier," she said. "I'm not going to sleep with you tonight." Laura smiled from ear to ear.

"Oh, I heard you; it's the furthest thing from my mind," I said, grinning.

"It's not that I don't want to, of course," she said. "I would just feel a little uncomfortable about my hair and all."

"I understand completely," I said, and I did, but I was thinking that she couldn't be more beautiful. I didn't care about whether she had her hair or not. I loved her for who she was, and my love was unconditional. I wanted nothing less than to make love to Laura, and I wanted to make her as comfortable as I could.

As we walked back to our cars arm in arm, we couldn't feel more right. I thought that we should drive over in the same car together, because I wasn't going to let her be alone in her car to second-guess herself for twenty-five minutes. I probably didn't need to be alone with my imagination, either. Again, Laura beat me to the punch.

"Why don't you drive us home in my car," she said, "and I will drop you off in the morning."

BINGO!

If for nothing else and, at the very least, the night would not be ending soon. I couldn't ask for anything more, could I?

So I drove us over the Tappan Zee Bridge to her place. I wondered what Laura was thinking—so many things were running through my head during the car ride to her place. We were so giddy—what a great feeling!

There was a familiar smell in the hallway leading to her apartment. It was the smell of home. It was a smell that I had forgotten after being away, but smell was a very powerful sense that brought me back home more quickly than clicking my heals three times.

When we got to Laura's door, I looked down at my key chain, without thinking, to find the key to open the door and then I remembered that I didn't have the key any more. Laura had to open the door.

The kitchen, dining room, living room—there were some changes, little things moved from here to there, but for the most part, her apartment remained the same. I tried to take everything in at the same time and got a bit dizzy. I looked for past remnants of me. There were a few, like the black antique iron that I bought for her when I was in Vermont with Paul as a symbol of her strength before our split. I did notice some pictures I took and the letters that I wrote to her on her desk, which made me glad. Ironically, there were more pieces of me in her apartment since I had been on the road than my belongings from the past.

My toothbrush was gone, but I was just glad not to see anyone else's in its place. Laura tried to make me feel as though I had never left. But I had been gone—lost time that could never be replaced.

Chapter 22

Love

Laura went in the bedroom to change into something more comfortable. I put my pictures down on the coffee table by the couch and went in the bathroom to brush my teeth. Laura told me I could use her toothbrush. When I finished washing up, I looked up into the mirror to find that Laura was standing behind me. Laura was just standing there, smiling.

"What?" I asked. But she just kept smiling as if she were going to say something but wasn't sure.

"What?" I asked again. "You have this little-kid smile on, like you're afraid to tell me something."

"Are you ready?" she asked, still smiling.

"Ready for what?" By this time, I couldn't resist smiling. With one quick motion, she grabbed the top of her head and whipped off her wig. There Laura stood, in front of me, completely hairless. I knew it must have taken tremendous courage and faith for her to bare herself to me that way.

I walked over to her, looked into her eyes and touched her face.

"I knew that you would be just as beautiful even without any hair."

Laura smiled, and we embraced. "Oh, Guy, you're crazy," she said and laughed.

Laura asked me whether I wanted to change into something, and then she reminded herself that my clothes probably weren't there anymore.

"I know the rules when we go to bed," she said. "Clothes won't be acceptable attire when we cuddle anyway."

"That's right," I said. "Rules are rules, and no exceptions or accessories allowed. Skin on skin, baby!"

We went into the living room and sat on the couch to look at the pictures. Laura only wore a nightshirt and a baseball cap. She already had some of my pictures up in her apartment, and I told her that some of the pictures I brought with me tonight were for her to keep. She was very happy.

I watched the way she looked in amazement and with pleasure at my photographs. Laura looked so beautiful. She looked up from the pictures and caught me looking at her. Our eyes locked and as I've told you, the eyes don't lie.

I caressed her face with the back of my hand, and then my lips met hers. Her lips were so soft and luscious, bringing back all kinds of memories. I wrapped my arms around her and glided my hand down to her knees. In the heat of the embrace, I knocked her hat off slightly, and we both smiled.

"I know that look, Guy," she said.

Lying poorly I asked, "What look are you talking about?" We started kissing again.

"You know what look, I'm talking about," she said.

"Well, what do you think?" I asked.

"I ... don't know," she said with apprehension.

"Well, I do know," I said with confidence.

I grabbed her hand and led her into the bedroom. The stereo already had the right music on. Laura had only one request, which was that we keep the lights off, not even light candles. It didn't matter much because the moonlight pierced through the slits in her blinds. So, it wasn't completely dark in her room anyway.

We stood by the bed and let our clothes fall to the floor. There we were, completely silhouetted in the masked moonlight. She grabbed my hand and put it where her breast used to be. I caressed her and kissed her.

"I knew it wouldn't bother you," she whispered.

And, it didn't—not even for a second. I wish she would have believed that from the beginning.

With all the care of holding a baby, I cradled her in my arms gently. I stroked the side of her face with my fingers as we looked deeply into each other's eyes in awe and wonderment.

We whispered back and forth, "I love you" and "I love you, too."

While we lay on her bed, we completely blended as our bodies became one. Laura was so soft and smelled so wonderfully. She breathed heavily as I kissed and caressed her entire body, not missing a spot. It was as though we were making love for the very first time—again. We called out each other's names in ecstasy; it was truly beautiful.

"This is the home I missed," I told her

"You're home, Guy," she said.

"Mmmm."

We spooned all night, turning with the grace of swans. I felt very different from the last time we had slept together.

In the morning while we still lay in bed, she told me that she wanted me to go back to the road and finish my journey. We both agreed that we still had things to take care of—Laura still had treatments to finish up, and it would be best for both of us. When we were done, we had the rest of our lives to be together.

It was a cloudy, rainy morning. It was the kind of morning that you could just lay around in bed all day and make love, sleep, order some take-out, and make love some more—a grazing kind of a day.

Unfortunately, Laura had to go to work.

"Ugh, what a lousy day," she said.

I smiled, laughing happily, "No it's not, it's the greatest day in the history of the world."

She laughed, knowing exactly what I was talking about.

While she took a shower, I stood in the bathroom doorway watching her silhouette behind the shower curtain, and my eyes filled with tears—perhaps tears of joy or tears of sorrow, most likely a bit of both.

I went out to get some fresh hot bagels, Mocha Java, and the *New York Times*—all a Sunday tradition. When I returned, we sat at the kitchen table enjoying it all when she noticed my Work Smirk coming on and she said, "Don't be sad, Guy, be glad!"

"I'm glad, I'm glad, I'm glad," I said like a happy child. And I was, I think.

Laura drove me back to White Plains and dropped me off at my car. We hugged, neither of us wanted to let go. We kissed and said good-bye several times. Laura started crying.

"Don't cry, smiling Guy," I said. "You will have puffy eyes and the red line will go around your lips."

She laughed while the tears ran down her face.

"Remember," she said. "This is not the same as the last-time good-bye." She was shaking her head while she said this, as though she needed to convince me. I wonder if she was trying to convince herself.

"I know, I know," I said. "I will be back, I told you that you have my soul, and I will be back for it. You are my destiny. Remember, such men dare take... I will be back to claim my destiny."

"I know you will," she said, this time nodding her head. "I love you." A tearful smile returned to her face.

"I love you," I said, as I tried not to let her see the tears roll down my face. She drove off in one direction, and I drove off in the other.

In the car on my way back to my parent's house, I could still picture Laura's smile as her head turned in slow motion to say "I love you" when she walked back to her car.

My tears of sadness to see her go quickly turned into tears

Love

of joy, and I felt like celebrating. I was on top of the world, and I wanted to share the feeling with everyone. I sang every song on the radio at the top of my lungs.

When I got back to my parent's, I danced all over the house with my sandals on. I called Paul. I figured he would spread the word faster than anyone else. Gabby was very happy for me when I told her about the night's events. I even told my grandmother the entire story. It was storybook material. I glowed, and everyone was very happy for me.

Don't worry, my mother, although prudently happy for me, kept me in check by telling me that I should still be cautious because Laura was still going through a lot. That was my mother's way, and she wouldn't be my mother without lending some heedful advice.

I told my mother that I didn't care what happened from then on out. I just had the best night of my life, and if nothing else ever happened between us, I could rest happy because I found out everything I wanted to know. All my self-questioning, all my speculation, was for nothing. I was doing things the right way, and it paid off.

I truly believed it didn't matter if we never got back together. I heard and saw everything I needed anyway. Laura loved me, and nobody could take that away from me, ever!

I know I will be back for my love, my soul, and my destiny.

The eyes don't lie.

Part VI

Conclusion

Epilogue

After Laura's treatments were complete she did end up moving to Boston to start anew—without me. It wasn't the way I wanted it, but Laura felt it was better that way. God only knows what goes through a persons mind in that situation. She knew her destiny… She was cancer-free for a year before she had to fight for her life again.

To be "worthy" of her insurance company's eligibility requirements for a costly experimental procedure, we put all hope in new drugs to reduce the tumors that had spread all over her body. Prayers seemed to be answered because the drugs worked and the tumors shrunk.

After the final drastic procedure performed in an attempt for a complete cure, Laura slipped into a coma and died a few months later. She had turned thirty-one a couple of months earlier. That's too goddamn young!

We traveled on some tough roads together before she died. I was lucky enough to have many conversations with her before her death. But the one that I had before she had a bone marrow transplant was the most I could have asked for. It answered all the remaining questions. When I think about Laura, I smile.

I have no regrets about the things that I've done in my life, I only regret the things that I didn't do. Go get it! Go do it! Don't wait for tomorrow!

It is because of Laura that I am the man I am today. She gave me the courage to leave when that was the last thing in the world that I wanted to do. She had the strength for herself and the strength to push me away to save my life. I became the photographer that she envisioned me to be. She gave me the strength to attack life instead of being afraid of it.

Her laugh and smile were contagious. Her zest, love of life, and enthusiasm were unmatched and became my guide.

Her spirit is alive in anyone who was lucky enough to be touched by her life. I am lucky.

God, I miss her.

AUTHOR'S NOTE

The Road Letters is a happy story, but it's okay to feel sad… Feeling is part of life—the good and bad.

Remember that there is always *something* you can do; after all, *doing nothing* is a choice—you're the one who has to live with it!

Breast cancer doesn't discriminate; it affects everyone. One out of every eight women will get it.

Someone you know will get it—your mother, sister, cousin, girlfriend, wife, grandmother, coworker, boss, employee, you.

Do something!

DISCLAIMER

This book was inspired by memories and recollections.

Names have been changed (no easy task) and some characters are an amalgamation of sorts. Some characters have been added or deleted out of necessity or whim. Some events have been compressed or stretched due to the mind's failings. Certain episodes are imaginative re-creation, and those episodes are not intended to portray actual events.

Why?

Some possible explanations: to confuse the innocent with real guilty people; because real people are ridiculous lunatics; because the actual fictitious people have very popular names and it would be to confusing to the reader; just because, and in no way is anything contained herein meant to cause harm, ill will, bad feelings, boo-boos, or malice to anyone.

GLOSSARY OF TERMS

- **Work Smirk**—A Work Smirk is the look you get on your face when you're having a great time at a raging party and realize that you have to stop enjoying yourself because you have to leave to go to work; a depressing, sickly, fun-and-games-are-over type of feeling.
- **FFFO**—Literally translated: Friends, Fuck, Friends, Over! We are a harsh bunch with everything game to be made fun of no matter how painful or hurtful it is. Subconsciously a way we can deal with difficult situations.
- **Bunker Mentality**—Bunker Mentality is when you have to settle down in a bunker and do what you have to until the war is over—no splurging, no extras, no fancy feasts—the salad days.
- **Kudzu**—a plant from Japan originally brought to the USA to prevent land erosion.
- **Spillway**— it's like puddles here and there that are always there, like a river but it's not, a stream but it's not; it's a spill way. Just water dotted here or there…
- *tude*—attitude abbreviation
- **Mo-Fo**—Motherfucker abbreviation.
- **Bubba**—is the term for a guy in Texas; hence, the president Bubba.
- **Sissy**—is the term for a girl in Texas; Debra Winger's name in Urban Cowboy. "Sissy, I apologize right back to the first time I hit you…"
- *Cuddable*—very cuddly.
- *Pantry Bitch*—Just as *Mise en place* in the culinary world means everything has a place in it's place, your position in a kitchen follows a strict hierarchical structure—you are what you are…
- **The Old Ball and chain**—lead weight that zaps every once of energy from you.

GLOSSARY OF TERMS continued…

- **FeenX**—phonetic spelling of Phoenix—the mythical bird.
- **Perfect bite**—The right amount of everything all fitting into one bite.
- **Scoochie / scooch**—a small unit of measure.
- **The Boys**—My buds, We can all count on each other for anything!
- **Snickety-snackity**—small plates you can nosh on while drinking
- **Krewes**—Teams of party supporters that get women to show their breasts by throwing cheap plastic at them.
- **Throws**—cheap pieces of plastic that girls will show their breasts for.
- **G-Ride**—Government ride, paid for by *OUR* taxes
- Tchotchke—a small object; a trinket.
- **Psychdog**—an exhilarating exclamation.
- **Bolo punch**—windmill motion misdirection sucker punch.
- **Ooofa**—exclamation of pain.
- **Blivet**—"10 lbs of maunre in a 5 lb bag."
- **Bloviating**—To communicate at length in a pompous or boastful manner.

CHARACTER LIST

Nick Anthony—main character.
Laura—Nick's girlfriend and the reason for this book.
Gabrielle—Nick's sister in law, head shrinker, confidant and CWN.
Joe—Nick's youngest brother of two and still going to college.
John—Nick's other younger brother, *Mr. Sensitivity*, out in the working world, and married to Gabby.
Nick's Mother and **Father**—enough said...
Paul—a very good friend from HS and confidant, *SSBtDiHPH*.
Richard—*Stoneman*, a very good friend from HS, owns his own business that his father gave him.
Jack Johnson—*Marlboro man*, a very good friend from HS, Federal agent.
Camilla—Nick's Uncles wife.
Uncle Charlie—Nick's Uncle and Godfather.
June—good friend of Nick's from HS.
Patrick—a very good friend from HS.
Jeffrey—Nick's mothers boss.
Carl—Nick's brother John's friend and salesman.
Will and **Ann**—family friends that moved away from New York
David—the Keed, a good friend from HS who moved away 10 years ago.
Karen—the Babe, David's wife.
Allen—Nick's cousin from New England that moved away from home.
Jane—Allens wife.
Daniel—Friend Nick met through Allen originally from NY
Liz—Laura's friend.
Mina—Laura's friend.
Ann—June's roomate in Atlanta.
Denise Macallan—First crush.
Danny Lupo—girlfriend stealer.
Shelly—Hostel worker.
Casey—Waitress.
Damn Dog—Allen and Jane's dog.
Silvia—Richards wife to be.
Pete's Sake—A person Nick never uses.

INDEX

W
Work Smirk— 1, 213, 217, 221, 236, 247
Will and Ann 98-99, 106, 121, 249

U
Uncle Charlie 68, 71, 74, 200-201, 249

T
The Old Ball and chain— 247
The Brady Bunch 43
The Boys— ix, 4-5, 20, 27-28, 106-107, 144-145, 195, 199-200, 203, 205, 228, 248
Tude 78, 247

S
Spillway— 93, 247
Snickety-snackity— 248
Sissy— 106, 247
Silvia 28-29, 59, 186, 203-205, 218, 249
Shelly 118, 180, 249
Scoochie— 176, 248

R
Richard 20, 25, 28-29, 51, 59, 94, 97, 106, 144-146, 167, 186, 203, 205, 249

P
Pete's Sake 9-10, 230, 249
Perfect bite— 165, 248
Paul 20, 28-29, 97, 106-107, 144-146, 167, 194, 203-204, 207, 209-210, 217, 230, 232, 237, 249
Patrick 55, 57-59, 61, 249
Pantry Bitch— 103-104, 247

N
Nick's Mother 249
Nick Anthony i, 47-48, 119, 142, 159, 161, 168, 170, 184-185, 189, 206, 249
Ned Beatty 181

M
Mo-Fo— 94, 247
Mina 67, 142, 227, 249

L
Liz 228, 249
Laura i, 1-13, 15-21, 25, 29-30, 35, 37-40, 52, 59, 62, 67, 73, 75, 78, 87, 96, 117, 121, 132, 137, 141-143, 145, 147-149, 158, 168, 175, 179, 190-191, 193-194, 200, 206-211, 213-214, 217-218, 221-237, 241, 249

K
Kudzu— 68-70, 247
Karen 60-62, 83, 249

J
June 53-61, 64, 67, 249
John xi, 39-40, 91-92, 106, 156, 201, 249
Joe 39, 143, 201, 249
Jeffrey 83-85, 249
Jane 150, 158-161, 165, 168-170, 185, 194, 249
Jack Johnson 218, 249

H
Hot as balls- 164

G
G-Ride— 248
Gabrielle 13, 201, 210, 249

F
FFFO— 4, 205, 247

D
Denise Macallan 164, 249
David 60-64, 73, 83, 249
Danny Lupo 164, 249

C
Clint Eastwood 69, 97, 109
Casey 132, 142, 148, 249
Carl 86, 96-98, 249
Camilla 68, 71, 201, 249

B
Bunker Mentality— 129-131, 149, 247
Bubba— 106, 247

A
Ann 55-57, 67, 98-99, 103, 106, 121, 249
Allen 109, 150, 156, 159-161, 168-170, 185, 249

ABOUT THE AUTHOR

Phil Ribaudo is a native New Yorker, but now calls California his home. He left New York in search of life, love, and beauty in America, and he found it. Ribaudo has led many different lives—private chef, schoolteacher, photographer, restaurant manager, entrepreneur, web designer, and writer. As a storyteller, Ribaudo draws from his life experiences and writes to entertain, inspire, and change the world.

Ribaudo travels the United States and Europe by car, plane, train, bus, and foot, photographing people, the countryside, and cityscapes as he finds them. He clicks away while traveling across the hilly terrain of San Francisco, down the streets of blustery Manhattan, up windy roads through canyons and forests, or strolling through the sounds of a jazz band in the French Quarter.

His photographs have hung in the corporate offices of Hewlett Packard, in the home of M. Scott Peck, and at the Cole Bailey Vineyards.

Phil Ribaudo is (the Irascible Chef™) and has worked as a private chef in San Francisco, the Palm Desert, and Mulholland Drive in Los Angeles. Like the ubiquitous Emeril, he is an alumnus of the world-renowned Johnson & Wales University.

Ribaudo is also the author of
The Princess and the Servant Boy
(currently out-of-print)

Information:
phil@ theroadletters.com
www.theroadletters.com

The FeenX Store:
www.theroadletters.com/zen

www.ingramcontent.com/pod-product-compliance
Ingram Content Group UK Ltd.
Pitfield, Milton Keynes, MK11 3LW, UK
UKHW041416180426
11947UKWH00007B/163